Chase,

Thank you Sooo....
Much for Taking the
Time to Read my Book!
You = Awesome !!!

ALEX SIX

VINCE TAPLIN

Thank you for reading Alex Six!
If you love it...
Please please please leave a review
On Goodreads & Amazon!
...AND TELL YOUR FRIENDS!
It is SO helpful! -Vince Taplin

When the devil had finished all this tempting, he left
him until an opportune time. Luke 4:13

Dedicated to my wonderful wife, Amy, for supporting me and taking care of our beautiful boys while I wrote this book. π

ISBN: 978-1-7348138-1-4
ISBN: 978-1-7348138-0-7
ISBN: 978-1-7348138-2-1

Cover design by: Vince Taplin
Library of Congress Control Number: 2020905601
Printed in the United States of America

ALEX

SIX

PR3F4CE

Her office was sparsely decorated with a pair of Route 66 signs and a painting that looked like it was created in the style of "Realism by 8-year-old." She sat behind a glass coffee table and motioned for me to park in a large black chair directly across from her. I sat, crossing my legs as I tugged on the hem of my skirt. I felt a line of missed hair on my leg, an annoying stripe only I could tell was there but will bother me until it gets skimmed.

"So! Here we are again," she said, resting her hands in her lap.

How should I respond to that cluster? I certainly didn't want to start the conversation. Not after last time. A long, uncomfortable pause lingered. She smiled at me while I smiled back. I could smell her perfume. It's cheap, probably something she picked up from a department store. Her suit was surely bargain basement, too; I could tell from the poor cutline on the shoulder and hips — clearly, she needs to charge more. She cleared her throat again and waited for me to speak. Some people describe a heavy silence as loud, which is bullocks because real silence is so quiet you can hear your heartbeat in your eardrums.

"Last time you were here..." She opened her notebook and skimmed a few lines. "You told me your husband has been acting strange. You also mentioned he has been seeing someone else?" My fingers picked at each other. Stop fidgeting and breathe. You can handle this.

"Yes. He has." Good. Good answer. See, you're doing a great job, no need to be intimidated by the ugly girl at the dance.

She wrote more notes. I could hear her pen scratching ink onto the page in the quiet office. I peeked around at her bland wallpaper and her small oak desk. On the desk, a variety of red, blue, and black pens sat neatly in a "World's Greatest Mom" mug. Does she have vodka in her bottom drawer? Does she tire of listening to problems all day, day in and day out?

Her pen scraped the page. "Do you know the woman?" she asked.

"I know her, yes."

"Does it upset you that he is having an affair?"

"He isn't cheating!" I felt my heartbeat behind my eyes again.

Moisture began to build along my brow. "He is just..." In my lap, my pointer finger quickly traced circles on a fingernail. "I don't know, experimenting!" I paused and adjusted my skirt again. "Once he finds out how much I love him, he'll love me."

"Do you think it's a healthy relationship if he is seeing other people?" she said and lifted her eyes from the notepad.

"No! Of course it's not healthy, but we've always had an interesting relationship. This is just... just... just another curveball. "Stop! Stop feeding her. Short answers, remember? Short, controlled, answers.

She jotted more notes. "Does he know you know about her?"

"Does he know? *Does he know*?"

I wiped my brow. My makeup was running, tears welling, mutilating my mascara. Control yourself. Don't let go. Don't lose control again. I forgot how hard it is to come here.

The therapist slid a box of tissues across the table. "Tell me about that."

Pins and needles in my mouth. I pursed my lips so tightly they went numb. I snatched a tissue from the box and wiped black smudges from my cheeks. How did this happen? How did this happen to *me*? To *us*? I hate him for it, but I can't live without him. His touch and his laugh and his... everything.

"We'll save that for later..." She scribbled on the page. "Does he know you're struggling? Taking medication?"

Words are trapped. My mouth opened but my throat was too tight to make a sound. My palms were wet. "No," I squeak.

"Last time you were here, you told me you felt invisible. Like his life is being lived without you. Do you still feel this way?"

My throat hardened around the spit I tried to swallow, like a snake squeezing my neck from the inside. Why are you pushing me, bitch? Stop! — "Yes..." My eyes met hers. Rage — sadness — Oh my God, I'm too vulnerable.

More scribbling. "Does he know about your condition? Your history? Your…" she began as she leaned forward, "…your mental health history?"

I see you.

I see you watching me from behind your coffee table. I feel your judgment. I know you. You're like all the others. *I seeeeeeeeeeee you. No!* Not today. "No, he doesn't know about my history." I'm so vulnerable. Why did I come back here? Check, please. Check, please! I'm done. *Done!* I should have never talked to anyone about this. Who do you think you are? You're a peasant therapist with certificates from a *state school* and a 2-dollar barn painting on the wall in the waiting room. I stood and walked to her side of the table. She leaned back with a smug, uncomfortable smile. "And no one else should know about my condition."

The knife felt sticky as it slid into her neck. Her eyes watched mine: predator and prey. She got too close — Why did you have to do that? Look what you've done! Why didn't you let me talk about him, or let me talk about my day and about how much I love him? Or you could have asked me *why* I love him. Or, or, or, or tell me that he will run to me and he will love me. He doesn't want that other woman. *I am the only one for him.* You did this to yourself, Counselor. You should have played nice.

She tried to yell but it was just bubbles and gurgling. "You don't know about my condition…" I pull the blade from her skin. "… anymore."

She slumped back in her chair, holding her neck with a goofy, surprised expression. You should have known I'd bark back, bitch. Her eyes turned off, leaving her with a final, dim, expressionless gaze. She looked pretty.

CHAPTER ONE

Professors never stop being professors, they only cease to have a classroom. I was no different. I'd taught at the University of Minnesota for five years when I was fired. Said I wasn't following curriculum, which is bullshit because their curriculum considered Watergate to be a recent scandal. I wanted to teach college kids to think, but the dean wanted them smart enough to think they're getting an education, but dumb enough not to realize they weren't. I taught calculus and business in the morning, general finance around lunch, and closed the day with a gen-ed class.

I'd graduated from the University of Wisconsin at the ripe age of twenty-two. Bright-eyed, bushy-tailed, and gullible. Recruited into the army as I walked out of the graduation ceremony.

I had a smile, a grad cap, and nowhere to be. Recruiters can smell that, before I could say "student loans" I was off to boot camp. My mind was sharp, street smarts dull.

Drill instructors could see I was green. I blushed, bled, and after being badgered, 1 became burly. Traded the soft touch of a college textbook for the cold pull of a trigger. I earned the rank of second lieutenant in the army and did some traveling. Saw the sights. Shot a few bad guys. Landed in a few hostile zones and ate a few hot dogs on other continents. After losing a few friends and killing some of theirs, I decided not to reenlist. I slid back into the civilian world and found the only job I knew other than strangling foreigners. Academics. The University of Minnesota offered me a job. They had a veterans program that put me ahead of the other pocket protectors.

After I was fired, I didn't know what to do. I was in a decent position though. The military still sent me checks for the bullet I'd caught in the shoulder. It didn't leave any long-term health problems, but they refused to stop paying me.

There had been a lot of bad press around firing veterans in the last few years so I received a golden parachute from the university to go away quietly. It wasn't enough to retire, but it was enough to pay down my house and put some money into a rental property. I embraced my new life and wore paint-covered overalls when I visited renters to fix their toilet or stove. I could solve complex math problems on any continent while returning gunfire, but fixing a busted gasket on a toilet seemed an ambitious adversary.

One afternoon while I was cleaning the lint trap on an ancient dryer vent, my tenant introduced me to her friend. A knockout. "This is Kraya, my friend I was telling you about…" My eyes met hers. Then they met her feminine neckline and gold necklace. Her neck jewelry naturally led me to her chest. I tried not to stare, but trying is overrated. Her waistline and hips were petite, legs immaculate and tanned under her skirt. I wondered what other treasures lie beneath. "So I thought I'd introduce you. Kraya, this is Victor." I tuned back into the show at just the right moment. She looked at me shyly, acknowledging my eyes dancing along her seams.

"Hi," she said. That voice. Ugh! Sultry and feminine.

"Nice to meet you, Kraya. Czechoslovakian name, right?" Of course I'm right, but I want her to know I'm more than a couple of ogling eyes and a pants tent.

"Yes. Wow. Not bad, Victor," she said with more confidence.

"Vick, please. My friends call me Vick."

"Are we friends, Vick?"

"I'd like to be."

I found every excuse to stop by the rental house. I mowed the lawn every other day and gardened for hours when I saw her car out front. I routinely came in for doorknob inspections and thermostat modulation tests. It didn't take long for us to start dating. We had a connection. A great connection. I could listen to her talk all day; of course, we never made it that long. The sex was good enough that I alone funded my chiropractor's coke habit.

After a year or so, she moved into my cozy two-bedroom house on the outskirts of Minneapolis. We talked more, fucked less — par for the course.

Anyone who expects the handcuffs and oral to maintain the same frequency after their girlfriend moves in has never had a girlfriend move in. The dogs playing pool were soon replaced with an abstract piece that "ties the room together." My furniture slowly migrated to the basement. My once dark, simple motif was replaced with what is now described as blossom white with "pop" colors, whatever those are. On her birthday, I gave her the present she'd wanted since she stopped taking birth control without my knowledge.

A bouncing baby took hold in her fertile womb. I was neither prepared for this, nor unprepared. It wasn't a money or responsibility problem, just an unforeseen obstacle. Keeping it was not up for debate.

I was smart enough to know not to touch that topic. Instead, I kinda poked at it from a distance with a stick — "We never did take that vacation to Fiji. We should, ohh, wait… We can't with the baby." I also left her a copy of *Cosmo* magazine with the headline: "It'll never be the same down there after the munchkin arrives." All these attempts were either ignored or misunderstood. Either way, he was coming.

November seventh. He arrived. I'd seen battle. I'd held dead friends. Nothing prepared me for the moment of birth. Both beautiful and disturbing. (Maybe disturbingly beautiful?) He stared at us with big blue eyes. I learned then what love is.

We were married shortly after. Her dress was beautiful, smile bright. My tux rented, fitting tight. I knew she was the one. My one. I'd been in love before — some overseas, some domestic. Some hot, some dull. But none compared with Kraya. Sweet. Gentle. Loving. Kind. Beautiful and sexy. She knew me, understood me, and hated me at times. Most importantly, she loved me.

We bought a few more houses and our rental business paid the bills. Most of them anyway. Our budget was tight, but not tight enough for us to have to budget for twenty-dollar purchases. I enjoyed the simple life. Married. Kid. Bills. A few cocktails at the end of the day. Sex twice a month. This is what people dream about, right?

The dream was shattered though. The day I met Alex…

CHAPTER TWO

Grocery stores are always busy. I often wonder who my fellow shoppers are. Do they work? Why are they wearing flannel pajama pants at one o'clock in the afternoon? Why are there seventeen boxes of fruit snacks, five bottles of Tylenol, and a can of generic baked beans in your cart? I reviewed my list, carefully designed by Kraya. Bananas, oranges, applesauce, asparagus, broccoli.

She caught my eye. She caught everyone's eye. Asianish, Russian? Something exotic. She was out of place, like a bicycle sitting in the first-class cabin. She had pants, or tights, or a dress — some striking pant combination I'd never seen. Tight tan leggings with bell bottoms and a biblical ass on the other end of 'em. A slit ran up the side of her pant leg.

I picked up my bananas and weighed them. Why do people weigh their bananas? Are they concerned with the additional twenty-six cents that extra banana would yield? It gave me a reason to stare through the scale to where she stood.

She wore a bracelet so dainty it made dental floss look like anchor chains and a necklace that shook glimmering stones as she walked. Her high heels clicked as she walked amongst the fruit. My first thought was how incredible the heels made her legs look. Secondly, why is she wearing heels in a grocery store?

Our eyes connected. Busted, dude. I turned back to the fruit scale, raising an eyebrow. I bagged my bananas and pushed my cart toward the pear section. Is it still a pear if there is only one? I focused back on my list: bread, dressing, those crunchy onion thingies. I continue reading, pausing occasionally to look down the aisle to make sure I don't trample other shoppers as I flee the veggie section.

I passed through aisle two and grabbed some spaghetti. One? Two boxes? They're on sale. But what is the normal price? Then I saw her. Standing in the middle of the aisle, staring directly at me. I decided to buy two boxes and threw them in the cart like a Frisbee. As I walked toward her, she blocked the aisle with a wide stance. I didn't mind the view, but why was she just standing there? I smiled politely and whispered, "Hi, excuse me," like any good Midwesterner would. She didn't move. If this were a two-hundred-pound man blocking my path it would be a completely different scenario. Why was she any different? Sexiness clause probably. My cart moves closer. She's *still* blocking my way. Move, ya hot broad, I have places to be, potato chips to buy.

"I'm sorry, if I can sneak by you here," I said, pushing my cart to her side. Why was I apologizing *again*? Because I'm in Minnesota, dammit, and that's how we roll.

"No," she said. Her eyes softened. She gasped and her lips gaped. A tear slid down her cheek to her shirt (or blouse or whatever that silky, sexy thing is). "It's... it's unbelievable!"

I'm only slightly less disturbed than she is.

"You... you look... you look *just* like him!" she whispered, a somber raspiness to her voice.

I smiled out of discomfort. "Miss? I look like... who exactly?" Did I mention she was still lost in a strange gaze — directed right at me? Or through me? It's the winner of the weirdest-shit-that-happened-to-me-this-week award. I took the opportunity to look her over once more — why not? I was close enough to smell the intoxicating, yet pleasantly light perfume she'd wrapped around herself. She stood motionless, staring at me. "Miss? Can I help you? Are you okay?"

"I'm sorry..." she said as she wiped her cheek. "I'm so sorry. You... you... you look like someone, that's all." She moved briskly by me, trading glances as she passed. She disappeared past the endcap of miniature toy cars and frosted cereal, leaving the light scent of her perfume and the diminishing sound of her heels on the tiles.

I carried on after she left the aisle. I needed peas. Green peas. What was she looking at? Did I pass the peas? Who the hell was she? Dangit, I passed the peas again. What was that all about?

I'd made a mental movie of the situation to tell my wife. I'd also recorded a few key shots to keep for another time altogether. Two hundred bucks later, I checked out and left the store. I pushed my cart through a few potholes before I remembered that I didn't recall seeing the vanilla extract in my cart. I scanned the receipt. I remember going down that aisle, and I swear I grabbed it, but... dang, I must have forgotten it.

Some would say, *Skip it. Go home.* Fools. You can't bake a decent cookie without gobs of vanilla extract. Kraya makes cookies every Saturday. Today is Saturday and there is no way I'm missing another cookie-Saturday. I loaded the back of my car with flimsy, overstuffed plastic grocery bags and ran back inside. I jogged through the familiar aisles looking for the vanilla while keeping an eye out for my mystery girl. I bought the vanilla, declined a bag from the pimple-faced checkout kid and left.

Could I still smell her? I drove, replaying the bizarre encounter. My flashbacks replaced with an empty lane, a green light, and a honk from the asshat behind me. I probably didn't run any red lights or sit at any green lights the rest of the trip home.

Kraya played with our kid in the living room. He laughed when I walked in. I used my leg to close the door behind me, hands full with bags of groceries.

"Welcome back! You missed the Carters. They stopped by with the baby," Kraya said with a smile.

She always smiled when people stopped by with freshly squeezed babies. Kraya didn't have baby fever, she had the baby plague. No matter how tired she was, crabby he was, or how many diapers we'd (really she'd) changed, she always wanted more. I was supportive of her infatuation with small, crying things. Even offered to get her another one someday, when the timing was right. She laughed. I didn't.

Most (smart) men get the joke. It isn't really up to us when we have babies. If we ever, for even a moment, believe we have any say in it, do this: think about the last time you didn't give it to her when she seduced you. Think harder. Remember? Neither do I. They own the show. You just coproduce.

I put away groceries and threw away the aging, wilting mess of carrots and other useless vegetables cowering in the back of the refrigerator. We made dinner together, played with the munchkin together, and put him to bed together. Watched Netflix and slowly crawled into bed together. I never found the right moment to mention the woman from the store.

I read my book, glasses on, with the bedside lamp coloring the room. The book was good, a hard crime book about a guy named Quarry. After about three pages, my eyes closed and the book slapped my forehead.

CHAPTER THREE

We were proud owners of several rental properties. I'd snowballed the debt and paid a few of 'em off. I found myself fixing something almost every day. Today, I was busy checking out what she described as, "Ummm, rusty water or something under the big round thing (water heater)." Not a good sign. That tenant was okay. Usually paid her rent on time. No parties and quiet(ish), but dumb as a box of short-bus rocks (not to be confused with public or private school rocks). I caught her trying to weed-whack a small tree once. Selfishly, I just watched. The tree, no less than three inches across, was "in my way" when she was looking out the window. Silly Teresa. Weed-whackers are for adults. I suspected drug use, or a mental defect, but landed mostly on drugs. Not hard drugs, just a bit of pot. I wasn't into it, but I didn't care if my tenants were. I'll take a stoned, responsible Cheetos addict over a mullet-sporting alcoholic any day. Usually the worst thing that happens with a stoner is a few grease stains from pizza or spilled bong water on the carpet. Both, unfortunately, have happened to this property.

The water heater was dead on arrival. It was spitting sad rusty loogies out the back, leaving a red trail from the heater to the drain. I killed the water line, drained it, and told her I needed to replace it.

"Do I like... need to pay for it?" she asked blankly.

"No. You, like, don't need to pay for it," I replied.

She seemed happy she didn't need to shell out any cash, but it was difficult to tell through the glaze. I cleaned up, wiping my hands on my cool I'm-a-landlord overalls. She walked me out. I gave her a cable company style estimate on when I'd be back to install the new water heater.

"I'll be back between noon today and tomorrow. It all depends on how soon I can order one."

Which was bullshit. Any goof with a credit card can pop over to Home Depot and grab a heater, some hoses, clamps, and get that thing installed in about two hours. But I'm no goof. I have things to do. People to see. Naps to take.

I left, heading south toward the clinic. My car was new. Not *new-new*, but new in the sense it didn't have rust and I'd only given it about five oil changes.

The streets were unusually busy for the morning. A few accidents on the highway were responsible for my tardiness at the hospital. I wasn't concerned. I'd probably spend most of my time in the waiting room anyhow. I'd received a letter informing me of my annual blood panel. These crooks take every opportunity to get a shot at another insurance payment. I parked, walked inside, and checked in with the attractive nurse at the counter. She was maybe twenty-five with short hair and a tattoo of a star on her left forearm. Was she hiding more tattoos? I'd put money on it.

After three minutes of waiting, a new high-speed record I might add, I was called to the first set of small rooms. Cotton balls, tongue depressors, and a bunch of tools that looked like pneumatic drill parts lined the small, sterile room. I sat on the butcher paper while the nurse checked my blood pressure. It wasn't the same nurse from the counter. This one was bigger, no tattoos or sense of humor. Just a curly haired mess of menopause.

"Do you smoke?"

Of course not. Not that I'd tell her anyway. I'd quit smoking a few times, but it always snuck up on me like a bad cold or an overdraft fee.

"Is your address correct?" she asked, but didn't look up from her laptop.

"Yes, ma'am." I'd recently learned *ma'am* and *miss* are a good differentiator of age.

"How much alcohol do you use, per week?" Lifeless eyes turned from the laptop screen to me.

"Depends on the week," I chuckled. She didn't. "Maybe three drinks per week."

She typed furiously. "Drug use?"

This time I didn't try to be funny. "No," I said.

"Sex life?" She stopped typing long enough to glance at me above her glasses.

"Good!" I mean... what else do I say here? Open-ended questions much, Rosanne?

"One partner? Do you have any concerns about STDs?"

"No. One partner. Married." I wanted so badly to ask her the same question. Ma'am, do you have sex often? I figured it was okay to ask since we're getting so personal. I imagine her living in a small apartment with her husband, Bill. He's a retired construction worker with back problems. She'd steal painkillers from the office sometimes to make him happy enough to fuck her. That's what she'd tell me, I guarantee it.

"The doc will be here in a moment." She rose abruptly and left.

It wasn't a moment. It was another ten minutes. So much for that world record. I was about to start playing with the blood pressure cuff when the doctor walked in. I stood, shook his hand, and sat back down. He introduced himself and explained what he was about to do.

"I'm Dr. Filstead and you're here today for a blood panel, correct?" He sat awkwardly on the side of the desk, peering into a file I was convinced was just a blank piece of paper.

"Don't ask me, I come when beckoned."

He smiled. "All right, let's getcha fixed up here…"

He lifted my sleeve and tied a rubber band around my arm. I made a ball with my fist and watched the needle poke into my forearm. I've seen enough blood to make a cheesy horror movie, but it's different when it's your own. He released the tight rubber band from my arm and filled the plastic vial. I felt blood slosh back through my veins.

"You should have the results in a few weeks." He smiled again, pulled off his gloves, and Larry Birded them into the nearby trash can.

"What are you looking for exactly?" I asked curiously. I realize I'm no spring chicken, but I'm no fall turkey either.

He flipped a few pages on the clipboard. "Says the works. Nice of your employer to get these done for you."

Employer? Our insurance was under our business. Must be another annual perk of paying premiums higher than most of our mortgages.

Next stop, a brand-spankin'-new water heater. It began to rain as I walked to my car. I love the smell of rain and the pitter patter of the drops. I picked up the pace and fumbled with the *unlock* button. The music startled me as I cranked over the engine. I flipped on the windshield wipers and as I was pulling from the parking space, my phone rang.

Unknown number. I answered. "Am I speaking to Mr. Miller? Mr. Victor Miller?"

"Maybe. Depends on who I'm speaking to." Every fourth call I received was some telemarketer. Or worse yet, an automated call with a high-pitched, enthusiastic robot girl telling me I'd won a cruise or the (nonexistent) warranty on my car was about to expire.

"I see. Mr. Miller, if this *is* you, I'm calling from Livingston Properties. We'd like to set up a meeting with you."

Holy shit. What does Livingston Properties want from me? They're a huge company, massively intimidating.

"Thank you, yes, this is Victor. When would you like a meeting?" I was hoping it wasn't another lot line dispute. I'd had all my properties checked thoroughly before I bought them. What do they want? A lawsuit? Fuck!

"Victor, are you open this afternoon? Four p.m.?" He sounded like a pretentious bastard. A cocky middle-management jerk who made less than he wanted but acted like the billionaires he worked for.

"Four p.m. today? Hmmmm... let me check my schedule." I crumped a sandwich wrapper. "Looks like I have some time at four, yes. Thirty minutes long, you think?"

"Mr. Miller, (sigh) I can't tell you how long it will take. I only set up the appointments."

Dick.

CH4PTER FOUR

I'd seen him before. Or had I? Sometimes people recognize faces of loved ones in strangers. Or fall in love with a smell or a taste before they see what it belongs to. I'm no stranger to love, nor is that first feeling of sexual infatuation foreign. I've had plenty of relationships and countless partners, but he is different. I feel like a virgin, realizing the first tingle of a strong fetish. This man. Oh, this man! How wonderfully he walks. His gait and his posture are thigh tightening. Did I hear a brave elegance in his voice? His masculinity is intoxicating.

I sat at the edge of my seat, fiddling with the stem on my margarita. Janet, one of the partners of Daddy's firm didn't notice him. She is babbling endlessly about the Waterman project. Only moments ago I was focused on her words, committed to its success. The profitability tables, overhead, and countless other expenses were on the tip of my tongue. And the carpenter and construction crew? Were they slow? Handicapped? What was wrong with these low-class citizens and their work ethic? They'd put this project behind schedule 3 times now.

A bead of condensation slides down the stem of my glass. "Pardon me a moment, Janet," I said.

She hushed and gave an understanding wave. "Oh. Yes, yes. Of course!"

My entire adult life I've been attacking opportunities instead of letting them slip through my fingertips. I wasn't about to let him slip through mine. I pull my napkin from my lap and toss it on the table.

I bump into half a dozen gossiping, backpack-laden college girls and dodged a skateboarding punk as I make my way down the sidewalk. I push through the crowd, trying desperately to keep him in view. My heart quickens as I round the cracked brick corner. He stops, looks at his wristwatch, and opens a tall door with peeling red paint. The neon sign in the window says NINE Tavern.

The bar sat snugly between a bookstore and a closed massage parlor. I follow him in, pulling open the door with both hands. This is crazy, but I can't deny this connection. I'm drawn, no-no, I'm *called* to him. I need to figure out who he is, maybe introduce myself? I need to. I feel it. I feel it everywhere. He has gravity — real gravity.

Is he a student? Doubtful. He is too old, maybe resting gently in his late 20s? Early 30s? I bite my lower lip. The door moans as I enter. It smells of cheap beer and expensive cigarettes.

He is sitting down at the bar, pulling out a faded stool with a creak. The bartender, clearly a college degenerate, acknowledged him with a nod and said something I couldn't hear. I take a seat at a table behind him, heart beating out of my chest. I can hear his voice clearly now. His words rumble with a sexiness I feel in my gut. A wet tingling begins to boil between my thighs. I can smell him.

He ordered a beer. As did I. I wait, too stunned to stand or try to communicate with him. I stare straight ahead, listening to his conversation and speech cadence with the bartender. The subtleties consume me. The way he laughs and the way he hung his jacket on the chair. The glimpse of his smile behind his jawline. I'm frozen at the table. It's been a long time since I've been speechless. Do I stand? Introduce myself? Bump into him and apologize? This isn't something I should struggle with. Stress drips down my pits into my dress. I pay them casually with a napkin.

I pull my phone from my purse, checking my makeup in the camera. I push the red circle, snapping countless pictures of him. Mostly his back, but a few shots of his profile slipped in there, too. I sip my beer, my disgusting beer. I can't believe people drink this stuff. I bet this is what those fucking construction workers drink while they slack on site. This is why they don't get anything done. They're drinking shitty, cheap beer. Animals.

I hear it. My luck keeps getting better. A sloppy, hunched kid, sitting a few stools down recognizes him. I focus every morsel of my attention on their conversation.

"Aren't you Professor Miller?" the kid said, leaning and spitting as he spoke. Clearly too many blue-collar beers for this redneck.

"I was." Professor Miller raises his beer with a wink.

His voice is a heavenly trumpet. What an exceptional, amazing, calm voice. I've never heard something so breathtaking. My hands are shaking, hiding below the scratched tabletop. Can I maintain my composure? Does anyone see me? Can they tell I'm sweating and trembling and so nervous I could vomit? I flash a peek over my shoulder. No. Thank heavens, no one is looking. The bartender is serving another glass of swill while Professor Miller watches a TV in the corner of the bar. "Nice to meet you, Professor Miller," I whisper under my breath.

CHAPTER FIVE

The Livingston Building was huge, not unlike Mr. Livingston himself. He'd amassed a fortune buying, building, renting, and selling real estate. I'd heard stories about him. Some say he's a cold, hard asshole. Others say he is a smart, cold, hard asshole.

I knew a guy, who knew a guy, who bought a few properties from Livingston. Said he was a ruthless negotiator and he always had food at meetings. He heard him say, "America's gotten too politically correct. Too wimpy and as soft as a grandma's titty. We should negotiate over a meal, like the Italians." Based on the size of his beltline, he must be negotiating fifteen hours a day.

The reception area was bigger than my house. Elaborate marble pillars climbed several stories. The stone floor was polished and shined. It took a while to cross the floor to the big desk with LIVINGSTON PROPERTIES, INC across the front. The desk shadowed the small receptionists behind it.

"Welcome to Livingston Properties. May I help you?" a gal with unnaturally white teeth asked from behind the desk.

"Yeah, I'm here for a four o'clock meeting. I'm not sure who I'm meeting or why." I smirked. "Can you figure that out for me?" She smiled back and clicked through some computer screens.

"Looks like you'll be on the forty-third floor." She paused, raising an eyebrow. "That's strange — it just says — *no further details*. You must be Mister…" she paused, scanning the screen, "Miller? Victor Miller?"

"I am. Is there anything else on the screen? Any more info? I'm not sure why I'm here. Is it a legal thing? Trouble with one of my properties?"

"So sorry, Mr. Miller. I don't have access to that information. Please take a seat and someone will be with you shortly."

I sat. The chairs were nice enough but left something to be desired in the rump comfort category. Figured with his money he could have sprung for something cozier. A fragile man in a slim suit appeared from behind a massive marble wall. He spoke quietly to the receptionist. Their mumbles echoed in the marble corridor. He turned to me, murmured back to her, and started his approach.

"Mr. Miller, a pleasure to meet you." He stretched a hand to mine. His handshake was firm. Practiced. His eye contact confident and his hands well groomed. He said, "If you'll follow me."

I did. I wondered why people never finish that sentence. *"If you'll follow me..."* What? What happens if I follow you? We strode past the bank of receptionists behind the big desk. I could see there were crowds of phones and security screens hiding behind that monster. We continued down an equally extravagant hallway. Endless paintings, hundreds of them, stretched down the endless passageway. The little man led me through a few snaking hallways to a platoon of elevators. He pressed the *up* arrow and entered a guarded passcode on the keypad. A pair of golden elevator doors opened. We walked onto the elevator and he pressed one of the buttons. It began to move. I coughed.

"Did I catch your name?" I asked.

"Oh, my apologies. I am Mr. Needle."

"Mr. Needle, do you know why I'm here?"

I'd bet you a nickel he didn't. He didn't seem the type to run the machine, only oil it. He shook his head with a shoulder shrug. We spent the remainder of the elevator ride in silence. The elevator chirped, then slowed. Plants, marble, and a windowless hallway slid into view as the brass doors opened. Mr. Needle extended a pointed hand, the polite, universal symbol for *"This is your stop, dude."*

I obliged and he didn't follow. The doors slid shut, sending Mr. Needle back downstairs to wherever he called home. I walked through the eerily quiet hallway to the only door at the end and knocked.

CHAPTER 6IX

Confidence has always been one of my best traits, followed closely by a methodical sense of analyzation. My fashion sense is quite impressive, too, but it doesn't qualify as an innate ability. Does it?

I didn't lack the confidence to approach Professor Miller. I could have done it. I could have turned around in my chair, stood up, and introduced myself. Sure, I could have, and it probably would have worked. I made the decision to improve my chances of success before I approach him. So I began to watch him. Surveillance and intelligence always add to the probability of success, right?

I watch him from the far corner of a coffee shop he frequents at lunchtime and sometimes I drive behind him when he runs errands. I hacked his password for his social media. I track his finances and monitor the profitability of his investment properties.

I even bought a home on his block and had it repaired for two reasons: 1) It improved the value of his property, and 2) I am able to slip in undetected through the garage and watch him work on the landscaping from the small, tinted garage window. He became a study. My study. My angel.

I met his renters, too. A yellow construction vest and a clipboard was all I needed to convince them I was official. I said I was with the Minnesota Department of Energy and the morons invited me inside every time. I keep notes on his schedule, where he was, where he'd been, and where my sweet was to be.

I have moments of doubt, too. Sometimes after I've been following him for a few miles, I laugh at myself and let him disappear into traffic. It's ridiculous. I'm being silly. Never have I had to try this hard. I'm not a stalker after all, just passionate.

I found his eBay account and I bought everything he listed. Everything. Unfortunately, he wasn't too active on eBay, so it never amounted to much. An old, faded leather jacket. A wristwatch inscribed with the words "*Congrats, buddy*" on the back. A few silver coins he said he's had since he was a kid.

I read the descriptions over and over. It offered a unique, rare peek into his world. A glimpse into his personal belongings, and his individual style. What is the story behind these items?

Why was he selling the jacket? And why is he selling the watch? Oh, the hands they'd touched. The intimacy they'd seen. I felt an odd twinge of jealousy because they'd touched Victor and I hadn't yet. I shipped the items to a freight forwarder in Denver to avoid being discovered prematurely. He'll know soon enough. My Vick. My candle. My stick. My rock. Drink up, love.

I took the time to befriend one of his renters. She was often high on drugs so it was easy to gain her trust. A few coffee dates and I solidified our friendship. Stupid girl. It appeared reasonably casual, but it took months for me to design. I wrote a meticulous plan to get the timing right. I calculated the date for perfect grass length and sabotaged her lint trap. Today was the day. He is coming.

I'd scoured the usual shops for the perfect dress, not too sultry, not too modest. A dress screaming femininity and whispering sex. I spent an hour in the shower, wore the best-smelling lotion in my collection, and got my hair and makeup done by Platinum Rosemary Shoppe, a high-end modeling and stylist boutique. I've worked out every day for hours. My tan is perfect. Skin supple. I'm ready, oh yes, I am *ready!*

I sent a text to let her know I was on my way. I checked my reflection in the rearview. Is that a blemish on my ear? Was that there before? Did I get a bug bite? Is it a new mole? A zit?

Blood rushes in beats and a light perspiration forms. I whip open my purse, digging frantically for my Tiffany blue mirror. I flip it open and examine the spot. It's nothing, just a shadow. I blow a heavy breath and put the car into drive.

Today I meet the man of my dreams for the first time again.

CHAPTER SEVEN

My knock was answered by a Mr. Needle clone. He was bigger, maybe older, but wore the same suit and sported the same smug mug. He opened the door and revealed a breathtakingly large office with a view of the skyline. Of the endless chairs, only three were taken. Backlit, dark bodies were featureless against the light from the windows. I enter, smile to Mr. Needle two-point-oh, and speak.

"Good afternoon. I have a four p.m. appointment. Am I in the right place?" I said. As I got closer, I could see more details of the two portly fellas surrounding a slimmer figure.

"You are definitely in the right place, Professor Miller," said the woman, whose features were still coming into light. "We've been expecting you with great anticipation." Her voice strong, and grew more familiar as I approached. A blue, form-fitting blazer hugged her chest.

Is it? It is. No friggen way. It's her. The weird lady from the grocery store. "I have so many questions." I'm doing that thing where I talk without thinking. Not good. I finally crossed the long room, positioning myself across from her and the two hefty executives. One looked to be about fifty, salt and pepper hair. The other guy older. And blacker. Skin, not the hair. His hair was grayish, too.

"We're sorry to catch you off guard, Professor Miller," she said and stood. The two puffy execs stood, too. "I'm Alexa Livingston." Her hand was soft. Smooth and sweaty, too. I leaned over the oversized conference table and shook the other hands. Theirs were less sweaty, but more wrinkly, drier, and shyer. "Thank you for coming downtown. I hope it wasn't any trouble to find." We all sat.

"No trouble. It's the only Livingston building on the block," I said.

"We've owned this building since I was a girl."

The pieces were coming together. She is his daughter.

"I've lived and worked here my whole life. It's a great place to call home."

"I bet it is," I said and shifted my weight in the leather chair. "I'd like to be blunt, Mrs. Livingston."

Alexa interrupted with an abrupt, "Miss. Miss, not missus." She then waved me back into the conversation.

"*Miss* Livingston. What am I doing here? Is it one of my properties?" I asked. I bet it's my flag street property. That thing has been a fucking disaster ever since I bought it." Or is it because of whatever happened at the grocery store?

"No trouble, Professor."

I interrupted *her* his time. "*Not professor*. That was a while ago." I shrugged. "Please call me Vick."

"Vick, I like that name. It's strong." I couldn't quite tell if her eyes were naturally seductive or if it was a business tactic. I didn't mind. She paused, letting stillness flood into the room. "Vick. I... I don't quite know how to say this." Oh shit. Here it comes. "I need a favor. And I'm willing to compensate you for your time and assistance." She shifted in her seat with wringing hands.

"You... you look like someone who was once dear to me." One of her blimps put a gentle hand on her shoulder. "You see... I lost my husband." She removed a tissue from her purse and wiped the wet from her cheeks.

"We were close, he and I. You look…" She took a breath and smiled. "Wow…" A few more tears and choppy breaths — "Remarkable! Just as he did. You two are…" She gazed to the windows, wiping more of the pain from her eye. "Identical. In so many ways. His eyes. His face…" Tears weren't tiptoeing anymore, they were pouring from her. "His hair…" She wept. The man on the right gently rubbed her shoulder, whispering something to her. She didn't whisper back to him. "It's all right. I'm all right. I'm so sorry; (sniffle) you… you are a gift! You (triple sniffle) could be his twin!"

As abrupt as a fart, she got up and left the room. Her sobs echoed down the hallway. Tweedledee lifted a thick leather laptop bag to the table. "I'm sorry about that. She is quite emotional about this matter." I noticed. I also noticed the skirt swaddling her hips like shrink wrap.

"Can you tell me what this is all about? I'm still not wrapping my head around it."

"Yes. I can understand your confusion." He paused, nodding to Tweedledum on his left. "Miss Livingston lost her husband last year. Tragic accident. Just tragic…" He pulled out a stack of paper wrapped in a manila folder like a taco shell. "They had a short, beautiful marriage." He licked his fingers, flicking through the pages.

"They were happy and had a dream life." He lifted his hands, implying the building and the Livingston wealth. "But there wasn't enough time to conceive a child." He removed a packet from the stack, held together by a struggling paperclip, and slid it across the table. He paused, allowing me the time to read the top line:

Sample known — Mr. Victor Miller — Donor Contract | Insemination procedure

Below the title on the third line, a number. Not a small one either, preceded by a dollar sign. "Mr. Miller. She is willing to pay you forty thousand dollars in exchange for your samples, waivers, and total confidentiality."

I always knew I was a handsome devil.

I flipped through the pages. I wasn't reading it; I was trying to act busy while the sparks in my brain tried to make a fire. I've heard a lot of stories and been involved in a few, but this was a cake topper. "Guys, guys... whoa, hold on here. Alexa Livingston wants me to be her sperm donor?"

"A *specimen* donor, yes." The black blimp could speak after all. "Miss Livingston would prefer this to be a quick, discreet transaction." He smiled. Great smile, too. Almost made me like him. "We wouldn't want this to become a public matter, Mr. Miller."

I suppose the headline "Heiress uses dude's cum to build clone baby of dead husband" isn't the press they're looking for. I opened my mouth, but only warm air came out. I'd never used the word befuddled, or even thought about it before this moment. Flabbergasted. Befuddled. Weirded the fudge out. All things I was considering while I casually perused the contract. "I need to think about it."

"You have twenty-four hours before the contract expires, Mr. Miller." Mr. Nice-smile sure wasn't giving me a lot of time. "We understand you are married. This cannot be discussed with anyone; unfortunately, that includes your wife, Mr. Miller."

"Hold on. How does this work exactly? Can you run me through this from the top?" I dropped the hefty contract on the table and focused my attention on the dynamic duo.

"I want a child of similar likeness to my late husband, Francis. You are astoundingly similar in every way." Alexa popped out from behind me. She seated herself to my side, a few chairs down. She slapped a photo of him on the table and slid it to me. I picked it up and cocked my head. She was right, we are alarmingly similar. A mirror. He had a few moles on his cheek and cooler, darker hair, but he could be my twin. I can see she's a woman of good taste.

Her eyes were still puffy, and I still couldn't peg her background. I'm sticking with Russianish. Definitely some distant genes from the Eastern Bloc.

She smiled. Quite a charming, dimple-filled smile. "I don't want anything from you, Vick. No parental responsibility, no visitation, no one would ever know but us."

"And the Olsen twins over there?" I added.

"And the Olsen twins. Yes." She slid the contract back to me. "Take tonight. Think it over. You'd be doing me a favor that would not be forgotten." As she leaned back, she crossed her legs. It would be nice to have the Livingston family owe me a few favors. The cash wouldn't hurt either.

"Can I assume attorney client privilege doesn't void the confidentiality clauses?" I asked. It would be purgatory to stay up all night reading this shit.

"Of course." She leaned over, snatched the nearby paperclip from the table, and pushed it back on the stack. It was holding on by a thread, like the buttons on her blouse.

Another question occurred to me that should have been asked a long time ago. "Miss Livingston, how did you find me after you saw me that day?"

"There it is." She pointed to Mr. Shit-eating-grin. "We thought you'd never ask. You aren't *that* difficult to find, Vick."

"How?"

"Easy, really. After I left the store, I waited for you. I sat in my car crying for nearly half an hour until you left. I took down your license plate and, voila! Here you are…"

Must be nice to have money. For a normal guy like me it would take a lot of legwork to track down a license plate. I'm guessing it was a phone call and sixty minutes for someone with her resources.

"Please consider my offer, Vick," she said and stood. "I hope to hear from you. My number is on the top page…" she said and circled it. "And the instructions are here." She circled that, too. "I can wire the money to any account, or give you a check or cash. It doesn't matter." She nodded to Tom and Jerry. They also stood and walked to my side of the table and extended their hands.

"Please do call if you have any questions or reservations."

I think they're done with me.

CHAPTER EIGHT

Another likeness of Mr. Needle helped me find my way out of the Livingston compound. Nice guy this time. Even validated my parking. My mind was swimming. Too many options, all of them good. One, tell my wife, get a green light or probably a red one. Two, keep it to myself, push the cash into my safe deposit box and trickle it into our budget. Or three, decline the offer, go back to my normal routine and try my damnedest to forget about the offer and Alexa Livingston's thighs.

First stop, my attorney's office. Going home wasn't going to happen, not yet anyway. I drove straight to the law offices of Robert Stik. He was one of those attorneys who had the cheesy commercial with the bad actor and the huge bookshelf. As I put my car into park, I saw him locking the front door.

"Rob! Hang tight. I need to talk to you." I got out quickly, hoping to catch him before he'd fully committed to closing. The rain had stopped but the sloppiness hadn't. I splashed through a few puddles.

"I'm closed. It's almost six!" His button-up was nicely pressed. He wore loafers and brown pants that looked a size too big.

"Fuck you, Rob. You owe me one." He did. We ran in all the same circles. He worked mostly in real estate, so did I. He drank beer, so did I. His wife's best friend was my wife's sister. That helped, too. He huffed, puffed, and unlocked the door. He flicked the lights on and sat behind his desk. I'd never noticed how small it was. Compared to Livingston's property, this is poverty.

"What is *so* important?" He checked his watch. I know he doesn't have anywhere to be so I dropped the contract on his desk.

"This officially qualifies as client privilege." I slid the stack closer to him. He flipped open the manila folder.

"What is this, Vick? Another tenant lawsuit?"

"Read. Tell me when you get to the fun part." I plopped into the wooden chair in front of his desk. He wedged a pair of reading glasses on his beak and pulled the page closer.

"Livingston? As in, Livingston the investor, *King* Livingston?" I've got him. He's hooked. You know you have a solid attorney when they read legal with a grin. He lives for this shit.

"*Alexa* Livingston, not Elvis. It's his daughter," I said.

He peered over his glasses. "Daughter, huh? I didn't know he *had* a daughter."

"Me neither."

"This is a donor contract. You know that, right?" he said and looked at me over his glasses. "She's going to pay you for your sperm sample? How the hell did you close *this* deal?" he asked.

"I had nothing to do with it. *They* called *me*."

He set the contract down and glared. "Alexa Livingston, from *the* Livingston family, calls you out of the blue, sends you a contract for your swimmers, and says, '*Oh yeah, and I'll give you forty large, too*' ?"

Close enough. I filled him in. The likeness to her dead hubby. The phone call and the grocery store stalking. He pulled the contract within reading range again. I told him, "I need to know what I need to know. Am I going to be liable for anything if I decide to go through with it? Any, you know, parental duties, child support, birthday cards? Anything I'd care to know before I plant my seed in the Livingston garden?"

He pulled off his glasses. "You can't go through with it, Vick. Kraya'd kill you."

"If she finds out, yeah, she would."

"Slow down, cowboy. This isn't a parking ticket you're hiding. This is forty large and a baby. You need to talk to your wife."

"I *need* to talk to my *lawyer*. The wife part comes later." I crossed my arms. I hate it when he gets personal, but the benefits outweigh the cons of having a personal friend as an attorney. It helps that he is cheaper than anyone else, too.

He raised his hands in the "don't shoot" pantomime. "All right, all right. I'm merely saying I think this is something a husband should talk about with his wife." He was right. But I could think of forty thousand reasons not to talk to her about it. She'd never agree to it. Rightfully so.

"Just read the contract. If anything puts me at risk, I'll say no." It was a good feeling to put this on his lap. If he says there are problems, I'm out. If it's airtight, I might reconsider.

"I can have this to you by next week." He stood, flicking off the lamp.

"I have twenty-four hours. Wait…" I checked the time. "Twenty-two hours to decide. I'll need it by morning." He grumbled again. His wife worked nights and their kids were still with Grandma. He had hours to play without anyone even noticing he was home late. "I'll double your normal rate, too."

"You mean, pay me my *normal* rate?"

"Triple. But read fast, asshole."

He nodded, turned the lamp back on, and got comfortable. It didn't take long for me to bore myself watching him flip through pages. All I could hear was the terribly loud, ticking grandfather clock he hid in the hall. I can't imagine how it doesn't drive him insane. Or maybe it had? I needed to get out of there, pronto.

It didn't take me long to say my goodbyes and get back on the road. The office was close to home. The drive, painless. After I pulled into the driveway and put the car in park, I sat there. I looked at the dark reflection looking back at me from the rearview mirror. Who is the man looking back at me? What will he decide to do?

Even as I slipped the key into the door, I was contemplating. I can't hide this from her. She's my wife. My best friend. But, I could do a lot for the family with the extra cash.

I turned the knob and was met with burnt smells, smoke, and the sound of whining fire alarms. Fuck. I'd heard the squeal at the door but I was too lost in thought to pay it notice. "Honey? Kraya? Kiddo!" The smoke was strong. Thick. "Are you here? Kraya! Are you okay?"

CHA9TER NINE

My phone buzzes and I open the text. "Sry for the late notice. :(An old friend stopped over. Mabz tomorrow?"

Who is this friend? A man? I pulled back into my parking spot below the building. Why is this person more important than me? I put a lot of time into this! The echo from my car door is loud in the underground garage. *Sorry for the late notice... Sorry for the late notice...* I read it over and over, looking from my phone long enough to dodge parked cars and curbs.

Click-Click-Cl-Cl-Cl-Cl-Click! I push the elevator button repeatedly. I know it won't speed it up, but it feels better. I check my watch, but fail to acknowledge the time, so I check it again. Finally, the doors opened. I leap inside, smashing the *close door* button with a closed fist. It takes years, *years*, to get to my floor. Frigging slow elevator. I paid to have these fixed last year, shouldn't they be faster?

This is preposterous. After what felt like another 4 hours, the elevator doors open to my apartment hall. I open the front door, throw my keys on the table, and unlock both locks on the door to room 9. This room has become my home. So many fantasies play within these walls. Once a walk-in closet, now a room dedicated to *him*. It serves a better purpose now than just another room in my apartment. I watch him from here. Track him and capture the beautiful, nearly imperceptible, idiosyncrasies of his life. I even went back to the NINE Tavern to get a number 9 from one of the walls to hang on the door — a memento of our first meeting.

"C'mon... C'*mon!*" The computers booted up slowly. Five computer monitors flickered to life, each containing a dozen camera feeds. After a lengthy startup, the cameras blink and show the view I dread. Professor Miller's car is parked outside her house. He is there without me. With a few clicks, the view changes to inside his rental house, specifically, the maintenance room. I'm so close to the screen I can feel its warmth. I turn up the volume. It *is* a woman. A skank. She canceled plans with me — for her?

I listen.

"Nice to meet you, Kraya. Czechoslovakian name, right?"

Is he flirting with her? My fingernail scratches furiously at my knuckle.

"Yes! Wow. Not bad, Victor."

Her outfit revealed too much. A stripper's version of fashion. But she is just another peasant; she may temporarily get his attention, but he doesn't want you. He will never want you. He is better than you and you know it. But... he seems to be taking the bait. You're smarter than this, Victor!

"Vick, please. My friends call me Vick."

You're getting too personal. *Stop*. My hand stings as I slap the table. I didn't realize I was crying. My face is as hot as a sunburn.

"Are we friends, Vick?"

She leaned into him with a flirty, sultry smile.

"I'd like to be," Vick said with a Cheshire grin.

I stumble back, falling to the plastic sheets on the bed in room 9. My throat is scratchy. My chest is tight. I'm dying. I think my heart is failing! This is it, look what you've done to me, peasant! I stand and punch the wall hard enough to knock the number 9 off the top nail. The upside-down 9 now a swinging 6.

I lie down, my heart still a mess of pitter patter. I wasn't there. *I wasn't there*! I set up the perfect meeting for *her*. That was supposed to be *me*!

CHAPTER TEN

I rushed to the stove. Charred remains of pasta, chicken, or soup smoldered in the pan. It popped and hissed as I chucked it into the sink. It's a miracle it hadn't caught fire. Or had it, but burned out? I twisted the smoke alarm from the ceiling and smothered it under one of the couch cushions to halt the shrill beeping.

As soon as the smoke alarm silenced, I heard it. Screams from the baby's room. My baby, my guy — wailing. Sobbing. I yelled for Kraya. My throat scratched from the belting volume. "Kraya!" What the fuck is going on here? I SWAT-kicked his bedroom door and found him standing in his crib, glossy red cheeks and puffy eyes. Gently, I pulled him from his crib, holding his warm body to my chest.

"It's all right, buddy. You're okay! Shhhhhhhhh," I said to him softly. His cries wound down, replaced with stuttered sniffles.

We navigated through blocks and books, making our way from his room. He was soaked in pee and tears. How long had he been in there? "Kray! Where are you?" I yelled. I checked the bathroom, the hallway, living room, and finally, the master bedroom. She lay lifeless on the bed. I set him down and jumped on the bed. "Kray! Kray?" I shook her hard enough to cause her head to bobble a few times before she twitched.

Her eyes opened, surprised. "Oh, hi, honey." She yawned. "You're home!" she said, rubbing the crustaceans from her eyes.

"Are you kidding? Are you fucking serious? You were sleeping? You left a pot on the stove! He's been crying in his room for God knows how long!" How did she sleep through the smoke? Or the smoke detectors? "What happened to you?"

She sat straight up, eyed the numbers on the clock, and wiped away a mouthful of hair. "Oh my gosh! It's past seven!" Frantic sheets flew from the bed. "I'm so sorry, I don't know what happened! I... I... I put him down for a nap..." She picked up the munchkin, hugging him like she hadn't seen him in a month. "I must have fallen asleep! Oh, gosh, I'm so sorry, guys." She held him. She knew she'd fucked up. It's one of those terrifying things about being a parent — realizing how human you are and that accidents happen. And they tend to happen in an instant.

We spent the next half-hour airing out the house, which wasn't cheap. The temperature was dropping. Minnesota weather was preparing for snowfall, lower temperatures, and higher gas bills. I could hear the ghost of my father saying something about *"heating the world"* and *"you wanna singlehandedly cause global warming?"* I swore I wouldn't be like him, yet, here I am counting dollars as they high-fived on their way out the windows.

The pan was dead. Either a day of soaking and another day of scrubbing or a drop in the trash. I opted for the trash. Pots are a dime a dozen thanks to cheap Chinese imports. Thanks again, commies. I was right — his diaper had overflowed. He had spent hours in that crib. Probably sitting and potentially some thumb sucking, but mostly lots and lots of peeing and crying. Poor fella. Tortured thoughts of what could have been kept creeping into my thoughts.

Wasn't long before it was bedtime. Some of us were more tired than others when the house finally warmed up. My little guy went down surprisingly fast. Kraya, too. I was left alone with my thoughts, staring at the ceiling. Since I'd been home, I'd been too preoccupied to think about the Livingston contract. It's a lot of money.

Is it dishonest? I know, I know — it's omission and one of those fucking white lies. I yawned. If the shoe were on the other foot, would I be upset? What, sell an egg for six digits and not tell me about it? If she put the money into the family, I say, *Lie to me, baby!*

But forty thousand — is it enough? Then it hits me. I snag my phone and blind myself as the screen flickers to life. I typed a squinted note for tomorrow and plug it back in. That will make the decision easier.

Tomorrow will be interesting.

CHAPTER ELEVEN

"You could make a submarine out of this thing." Rob sounded like he was in a jar. "It's airtight."

"Am I on speaker?" I usually am. Rob tends to put me on speaker and pace the room as he talked. I heard a few crunches and a click.

"Is that better?" It was. "Good. Yeah, I read it. Twice. They spent some time on this one, Vick. It's solid."

"What do I need to know?" I'm not sure how to take the news. Is it good or bad that Rob didn't make the decision for me?

"Nothing. You are literally only there to spank it, crank it, and leave it. You get paid and they never contact you again. But there is one thing..." Paperwork shuffled.

"There is an adult contact clause. If child A, at any point contacts, makes notice, calls, writes, visits, blah, blah, blah, at any time, you are subject to a one million dollar claim. If aforementioned occurrence arises, Child A has, or will have, been told he was conceived from a frozen specimen from no less than ten years prior to the design of this contract."

"In English, Rob." It was challenging enough to drive and talk on the phone.

"My interpretation is if the kid ever *does* reach out to you, they'll give you a million bucks *and* they'll say it was from a frozen sperm bank. It means you donated long before you and Kraya were married."

I shrugged even though no one could see it. "Not bad." It was a good insurance policy if Junior ever made his way to my door. For a million bucks, I'd bet they'll do their best to keep him from wandering. "What else?"

"Honestly, it's a pretty good deal. You're not responsible in any way. You aren't legally able to even see him if you wanted to. No child support. No liability if she doesn't get pregnant." He laughed. "There is even a quality of life guarantee. Lucky bastard gets *fifty million* on his eighteenth birthday."

He rambled for another minute or two, noting a few other high points. He covered how the money would be paid and a timeline of events. They even included a custody chain if Alexa were to die. Every angle, no matter how insignificant, was covered. At the end of the conversation, he laid on another classic Rob guilt trip. He told me I should tell Kraya. Involve her.

"Would you take the deal?" I asked him.

He paused. "Never. I'd never betray Sarah like that. No way."

"Even if she'd never find out? And if she *does* find out, you get a cool mil and have a rock solid alibi?"

"I think it's trouble, Vick. A slippery slope. Today it's sperm donations, tomorrow it's stealing the coins from the penny jar. I'm telling you, dude, just tell Kraya."

We agreed to disagree. I was fine with it because I hadn't made up my mind. Not entirely. Before we hung up, we talked about the kids, work, my Twelfth Street tenant, and a few other things. Now that I know the contract is tight and I'm not signing away my firstborn, I dialed the number. Alexa answered on the first ring.

"Professor, I knew you'd call," she said.

Arrogant much, Alex? "Oh, wait, is this the Pizza Palace?"

"You've had time to review my offer. I hope you're calling to say yes."

It occurred to me late last night, right before I fell asleep. Never leave the car dealership without negotiating. It's Sales 101, for God's sake. "I appreciate your offer. I'd be more interested if it said sixty thousand. If you'll adjust your contract, I'll reconsider." Once again I'd managed to push my decision on someone else. Since Rob didn't put the kibosh on this thing, maybe she would. I was about to find out if I had big stones between my legs or if I had bigger stones between my ears.

"You're feistier than I expected, Professor," she said.

"Vick, Miss Livingston. Just Vick."

"*Just Vick*," she said, then paused, releasing a heavy sigh. "I'll accept your offer for sixty thousand and sweeten the pot by offering a five-year membership to the Orchard Path Golf Club. But this offer is only good right now. Are you going to make me a happy woman? Or disappoint me?"

What a funny thing to say. She opted for pressure, and the worst kind of pressure, too. The emotional pressure that puts me in charge of her happiness or her disappointment.

Thankfully, I'm good under pressure. "As for your disappointment or happiness, that's between you and your shrink." I chuckled to myself. "But I'll sign."

"Yes? Yes! Great! Yes! Wonderful! The instructions are on the packet. I'll have a new draft written with the new dollar amount. Can you still make it on time?"

It's a bummer I can't brag about my negotiating skills tonight over the dinner table. *Honey, guess what? I negotiated an extra twenty grand today with that hot Livingston broad. All I had to do was beat-off in a cup, and boom, our college fund is back in action.*

"My attorney still has the contract. Can you give me the details again?" I said. She gave me the details and I wrote them on the side of a coffee cup. It's nice to hear someone this happy — to *make* someone that happy.

I was looking forward to seeing her, and giving her something only I could give. It felt, I don't know, selfless. Chivalrous? Fuck, who am I kidding? I wouldn't do it if she didn't pay me. Would I? I pondered that for a second. No good answers behind any of those doors.

"You're going to give me something I've wanted for a long, long time, Vick. Thank you. See you in a bit."

Looks like I might be giving her a little bastard after all.

CHAPTER TW12VE

I watched in horror as months turned to years. Kraya, that fucking bimbo used some voodoo peasant magic on him. She'd tricked him — I can see it. It isn't real. *It isn't real, Vick — she's a farce!*

I watched them eat breakfast. I watched them talk on the porch. I watched them get drinks and laugh. And I watched them have sex. *Something will happen. Fate will intervene. He will love me.* I say these words many times a day in the small mirror in the corner of room 9.

I record their lovemaking sessions, isolating the parts of the video with just his moans and body. I've captured a full, blissful hour and 26 minutes of just Vick's torso, writhing and grunting. I play it every morning as I lie on the plastic sheets in my tiny room.

Sometimes he stares up at the camera in the ceiling. Can he see me? Does he know I'm cumming with him? ...to him?

He knows, underneath it all, he knows me. He feels my love and my desire and my passion and my yearning, oh my yearning is strong for you, love. Month after month it gets stronger. He knows I'm here waiting and watching. I'm his angel in the wings.

I hoard everything he sells on eBay. Personal effects like more shirts and a bike, as well as a box of hats and his old golf clubs. Some of the hats still smelled of him. I'd amassed a great collection of his treasures. Every time I touch his shirts, my legs quiver. What power you have, Professor. What power indeed.

The manikin in room 9 bares his watch, jacket, jeans, socks, and undergarments. I began sneaking into their house to borrow things, an activity that grows more exciting by the visit. Things like boxers and hair clippings, handwritten documents and photos. Items he would never miss — possessions I can't live without. When I feel extra raspy I put cayenne pepper in his wife's panties or steal her credit cards. I hope the missing items will spark controversy between Vick and his wife. They rarely do.

Next to my professor manikin was a blue Tupperware chest filled with vibrating phallics and insertables. My prized toy is a replica of what his member looks and feels like.

It took me hours to analyze the videos and send all of the right angles to the manufacturer. A small fortune spent for a replica penis is a good fortune spent. He'd be so flattered to know how many hours he's been inside me already.

I found out why I stopped finding wet condoms in the trash. She is using birth control pills now. I found them in the bottom drawer of the nightstand. She is sloppy though. Figures, peasant bitch. She probably can't count. I started noticing pattern holes in the birth control dial. She's skipping days. You cunt, you crooked cunt, what typical trailer park games you play. She was going to trap him and once she does, she will control him.

I visit almost every night while they sleep. Their alarm code is their anniversary. I crush birth control in her protein shakes, hoping to counteract her attempts. But I failed. How could I be so stupid? Had I not put enough in or did she stop using the shake mix? I watched as she told him about her missed period. I *fucking* watched, *live*, from the same hidden ceiling smoke detector camera.

I sobbed and scratched uncontrollably at my thighs. I rubbed my skin raw and my middle fingernail snapped off. The words "I'm pregnant!" echoed through my speakers.

"I'm pregnant!" The world is dizzy. "I'm pregnant!" I'm glued to my chair in horror. "I'm pregnant!" Moments ago room 9 was comfortable — now it's stuffy and claustrophobic. Her plan is working and mine is failing. "I'm pregnant!" *How* did this happen? "I'm pregnant!" Am I losing my edge? "I'm pregnant!" I've always believed I'm more intelligent...

I've underestimated you, Kraya the peasant.

I slapped myself hard enough for my skin to burn and swell. Again and again I pummel my deserving face with a closed fist, an open palm, and a slap that echoes like a lightning crack. I hug the manikin and cry in his arms. Snot, blood, and tears stream down my face onto his jacket. His scent is so fresh. I kiss his photo and whisper, "You will be mine, Vick. Hang on, Vick. I love you. I'll straighten this out. I need to take this further..."

CHAPTER THIRTEEN

Livingston Tower had its own grocery stores, toy stores, bars, and chiropractic offices, so it wasn't a surprise they had a clinic, too. I parked three or four rows from the main entrance. The chilly weather was beginning to bite. I rarely have gloves, never a hat, and my jacket is usually two seasons behind, which makes me the second worst prepared Minnesotan in the state. I entered the cavernous lobby again and greeted the receptionists. Why did they build the desk that large? If it's an ego thing, it's working. I can tell where I am and who owns the building. Kudos, marble salesman.

"I have an appointment with…"

"Me." Alexa approached from a nearby hall, echoing with her clicking heels. The receptionists stood straighter. Typed faster. The blonde one smiled so wide I could tell she needed her wisdom teeth out. "Welcome back, *Just Vick*."

What is it with this woman and these slits that run up the side of her dress? She asked me to follow her and she took the lead. There is something different about her. Kinder isn't quite the word — more personable? Just... different. Or am I different? Nah. I'm still me. Except now I'm walking behind Alexa Livingston. Rather, watching her walk. Her legs slid into a tight, slender torso that swayed on her step. This is exciting, but I know as soon as I deliver the goods I'll be evicted and forgotten, not unlike so many of their tenants. What's the difference between me and the others? I'll be discarded with sixty thousand and access to the finest golf club in the state, the gold standard in golf and lounges. Even in the throes of winter, the richest geezers gather for morning coffee at the club. Anyone who had a few commas in their bank account is a member. Or wants to be.

We made our way through the Livingston labyrinth and found the elevators behind an elaborate fountain. She entered a code on the brass button rack like Ol' Needledweeb. Her dainty fingers dialed one-one-three-zero, then selected floor forty-four, one floor above where we met yesterday. I wonder what those numbers signify? I know it's Winston Churchill's birthday, November thirtieth (a fact that was drilled into me by my balding seventh grade homeroom teacher with gingivitis), but she doesn't strike me as a history nerd.

"We…" Alexa stutters. "We'll need to stop at my apartment first. My lawyers drafted a new copy and should have it finished and waiting." Her eyes focused on the digital numbers as we passed floor twenty, twenty-five, etc. I nodded. Our eyes connected awkwardly followed by shy smiles. She is an interesting bird.

"Oh, yeah. No problem," I said. I always enjoy seeing how other people live, especially rich folks like her. I wonder what her place looks like… Is she secretly a My Little Pony collector? Or a hoarder? I'd put money on her being a red wine drinker, and I'd double-down on her having a sign that reads something like "*Live, Love, Laugh*" in squiggly cursive.

We exchanged a few casual remarks, mostly about the weather. She pulled a strand of hair from her forehead and tucked it gently behind her ear. She knew I was watching. She must know; these fancy broads can feel it. Her neck, too, strong, polite, feminine, and inviting. I'm glad I am married. If I wasn't, I'd never sleep again. I made a joke about her commute to the office. She's the only person I'd met who lives a floor above their office. Must be rough.

"It's quite nice. But it can feel a bit isolated. I can spend weeks, sometimes months inside this tower. Easy to forget the outside world," she said.

The elevator stopped, dinged, and the mirrored brass doors opened. Another set of doors stood alone in a tight hallway. She entered one-one-three-zero on another keypad next to the knob. The same code.

She opened the door. I'm met with a landscape view so sprawling it made me dizzy. It smelled of new carpet and kitchen cleaner. Not a hoarder — not even close. The apartment was sparsely decorated with lots of rooms and plenty of doors, many closed. One of the rooms had a number on it. Hard to see from way over here, but I'm pretty sure it was a five. Probably a maintenance closet.

I popped my head into the bathroom. It too had floor-to-ceiling windows overlooking the city's buildings and parks below. Next to the tub was a set of gold faucets and a bidet. Gaudy for my taste in places to poop, but impressive.

The living room was massive with recessed flooring and perfectly spaced couches, all white, clean, immaculate leather. Empty coffee tables and lonely books on shelves peppered the room. Lots of stainless steel. Plenty of glass. Not a hair out of place, or a kernel of dust. Like a game show host's assistant, she pointed to her space. This chick's as neat as an autistic librarian.

"This is it! Cozy, but I love it."

Cozy? As in, small and homey? I think she's been in this tower too long. My entire home *and* the land it sits on would fit in her living room. I followed her into one of the back rooms where she offered me a seat. It had a desk, computer, and a white cup containing a cluster of new pens. She opened her laptop and typed a few passwords.

There I am, staring back from the wallpaper on her computer. Her husband, my likeness, graced her screen. I'm not getting used to this. I was staring back at myself from a few pictures on her desk, too. And several more from the walls. Pictures of my clone at the beach, holding onto Alexa's waistline and a cocktail. There I was again in Paris, standing next to her at a fancy restaurant. Over there, I saw myself shaking hands with someone, likely her father from the size of his belly. It's weird. Cool, I guess, but weird. His good genes were about to pay my bills. Thanks, dead guy.

"Shit, it's not here yet." Agitated, she typed a note to someone, presumably her lawyers. "I pay them enough, you'd think they could send things on time." Yep. Lawyers. Can't live with 'em, can't kill 'em. They'd start suing you before you could reload. "I'm sorry, it'll be a few more minutes. Can I show you around while we wait?" I obliged. We started at the kitchen. She offered a bottle of water and I took it. She then told me about the imported granite and her European appliances.

I was right about red wine. She had a temperature-controlled wine fridge. The dining area was nice, but a pinch too sterile for my taste. A massive table held twenty-two spots, all with plates, silver, and a few glasses. It looked as if the tags were pulled off yesterday.

One of those goofy celebrity magazines lay crookedly on the side of the couch and a cup of coffee rested nearby. So far, it was the only sign of life in that place.

We wound our way to the other side of the apartment. We skipped the maintenance room with the number six on the door (wasn't a five after all) and entered a storage room. She scoffed at the clutter, although I didn't see anything out of place. My idea of storage meant stacks and leaning piles of old shit. Hers was colorfully organized Tupperware bins.

Just as I was about to leave the room, a small reflection caught my eye, a tiny camera in the corner. I looked back to the living room. There, too, mounted high in the corner of the room, tiny cameras watched. I asked her about it. She laughed. "My husband and I liked to travel. We had them installed to watch the dogs while we were away." Dogs? I can't imagine an animal ever being in here. If it were, she must have hired a forensics team to pick up every dog hair with a tweezers.

We walked into her bedroom; rather, *she* walked into her bedroom. I stayed near the door like a gentleman. She wandered through the room, telling me about her French bed frame and Norwegian makeup chair. How long had it been since I'd been in another woman's home, let alone her bedroom? A while. Quite a while.

Eighty-some pillows lay on her bed. This room smelled of a nutty vanilla, and of course, more of that fruity, sensuous stuff. A few more of those pictures of her croaked husband stood next to the bed. Another beach shot. Pink bikini this time, shrouded by one of those designer booty scarves women loved to wear around their waistline. Poor bastard. I bet they had some good times in here. Which reminded me to look around for cameras. No luck. At least she had *some* sense of privacy. Or her pups did. Whatever.

Scattered bottles of makeup and other feminine elixirs littered a desk on the far side of the room. Cotton balls and lipstick lay haphazardly. Everything else in her lair was perfectly orderly. I have a theory that no woman has the ability to maintain a clean makeup section. This now, is proof.

Her phone buzzed. Gentle fingers scrolled on the screen. "Ah, the contract is here." A printer roared to life in the nearby office. I was relieved to get the hell out of that bedroom. Too many ideas that would land me in divorce court.

Pages pumped from the printer. Seemed endless. I waited, eventually sitting back in the seat I'd been in before. She pulled the first stack from its hopper. "The adjustments are here." She pointed. "…and here in red. The dollar amount and the club access have been added." She leaned closer. The smell of her hair was intoxicating — a bouquet of femininity. She leaned in such a way the fabric rested to one side, revealing two tanned mounds. I focused back on the contract; I signed and initialed. Signed again, and put my initials on a few more spots. Mortgage paperwork is less demanding.

After I signed the last page, Alexa said, "Oh, I did add one thing." She smirked. "I didn't think you'd mind."

CHAPTER 4OURTEEN

I have a distraction. I've made a new plan.

Francis is perfect. A New York State alumni, stockbroker, and exemplary example of my level of society. I found him on an exclusive dating site. He had enough money to travel and enough sense to know he should.

I met him on the tarmac. His father's plane wasn't as large as I'd been told. We wined, dined, and spent the evening in my apartment on the 44th floor. We avoided everyone, taking cargo elevators and private cars to and from. No need for gossip and no need for anyone else to know about my fling with Francis.

The seduction was easy. He was ready before he'd even met me. We were a perfect match. Beautiful. Wealthy. Fun. Everything was perfect except for that wretched East Coast accent. Can I mold him into the person I need him to be?

We started meeting every weekend. Usually at a resort or distant destination. I laughed at his jokes and I fucked him like he was a god.

Three months after we met, he proposed. It wasn't out of the blue or too fast for me. I'd dropped hints, leaving plenty of notes about spending our life together and I read "bride to be" magazines by the pool. I said yes, gasped, and threw myself on him.

We were in Spain when he popped the question. I sent emails and made all of the obligatory phone calls. Everyone was excited. Even Mother showed a glimmer of happiness behind her heavily sedated eyes. She still took pills. She still drank and she still slept more hours than she was awake.

We toured Europe and planned a magnificent destination wedding a few weeks out. Daddy flew over but the rest of the family didn't. Francis's parents came, too. They wanted to meet the vixen who stole his heart. I could tell from the Skype conversations that they didn't approve, but what could they say? He's a grown man. A handsome, rich, young, grown man.

The wedding was small. Very small. Just the parents, less my mother. It took place on a beach in Ireland. The hotel was beautiful. It didn't matter that it rained on my white dress. I smiled and cried — all the things a bride should do.

We honeymooned and returned to Minnesota to stay in Livingston Tower a few more nights before we decided where to move. He was ecstatic. I was his fantasy, his super bride. All woman, all sexual, brilliant, wealthy, and all loving.

We still avoided the main elevators. It'd become habit. It was exciting, living in secret, making the world wait to see who I'd picked. No one in the building had met him. My plan: to have a grand reveal to the family, friends, and other wealthy families next week. Daddy spent so much time (and money) planning the welcome home reception.

The first night home I made him feel like a man. I am his wife, a trophy to be played with. We stayed naked all night, rolling and tossing with labored breathing. Once our bodies finally had had enough, we twisted together to rest. Bottles of empty champagne littered my room. He snored, drunk and asleep.

But I was not asleep.

CHAPTER FIFTEEN

"What is the change?" I picked up the stack, flipping through it like I knew what the hell I was doing.

"Oh, it's nothing. A quick meeting. We'll need to meet again in a few days to go over your family ancestry. You know, things he or she may ask down the line." She took the contract from me, sliding it into an envelope with a thud. "Standard practice."

Seemed legitimate. "I can do that. Probably a good idea. The kid'll ask someday where he came from." Besides, my family history was short. Mom and Dad were pretty vanilla. Grandparents from somewhere Nordic. Easy peasy.

We found ourselves back in the elevator, heading down to the clinic on the twelfth floor, creatively named The Twelfth Floor Clinic.

"Good luck down there, Vick. This means a lot to me."

I felt a soft hand on my arm. Her arm remained for longer than a tap, but shorter than a power-play handshake — you know the one.

I smiled, staring into those damn eyes again. "Means a lot to me, too. Glad I can help, Miss Livingston." Shit, yes, I'm glad to help. I'm thinking about a trip to Disney. And at the end of a long day, I might just go hit a few balls with other socialites.

"We're past *Miss Livingston*, Vick. Call me Alex. You're about to father my child after all."

I suddenly felt sick to my stomach. Those words were sharp. Kraya would be *so* hurt if she knew what I was about to do. So many conflicting voices raced through my noodle. My decision had seemed so obvious. Now it felt more like cheating — a painful violation. If Kraya ever found out, it'd go over like a box of chili-flavored tampons. But, it might be too late now. The contract is binding and I signed the thing. I can't imagine what her legal wolves would do to me, *do to us*, if I backed out now.

Get in, get out. Get paid. Forget about it. I offered Alex a halfhearted grin. "Okay, Alex." What else can a guy say here? This wasn't in the manual.

The clinic was accompanied by a pharmacy, a quaint bookstore/coffee shop, and a few other stores. Phil's Ice Cream Shoppe and the Wing Shack also flanked the sides of the hallway.

The clinic had a massive logo above the row of glass doors. The neon sign was a big number twelve with the word *clinic* running vertically up the inside of the number one and a small "*The*" in cursive above the twelve.

Alex was nervously wringing her hands. "Well!" She paused, smiling widely. "This is it, Vick." She pointed to the clinic. "Dr. Vanberg is waiting for you." A thin, white-cloaked man stood near the entrance. Again, she touched my arm, this time with a few gentle squeezes. "I'll be thinking about you." This broad is something else.

I spun my phone on the tips of my fingers. "Oh!" Alexa gestured to my device. "I forgot my phone upstairs. I need a picture of our big moment. Do you mind?" I lifted the phone and unlocked the screen. I tapped the camera icon and snapped a picture of her.

"No, of us! Today isn't about me. It's about us, making something magical. Something special." I cocked my head. About *us*? Funny. She approached from my left, wrapping her arm around my shoulder. Her face, so close I could smell her breath, sweet and minty. Her hair whipped to my side like a shampoo commercial. I wrapped one arm around her waist and with the other, held my phone at arm's length. Her stomach is warm, hard too, moving with her breaths.

I snapped the picture and clicked a few more times to make sure we got the shot. "Can you send those to me? You have my direct line." I did have it. She'd circled it on the contract.

"Sure. As soon as I..." I wanted to say *as soon as I'm done beating off in the room back there, I'll send it,* but I opted for tact. "...am done in the clinic, I'll send it over."

"Please!" What is it with her and touching my arm? "Please send it now." Her voice controlled. Serious. Apparently she wanted it now, like, *right now.*

"Yeah. Can you give me your number again? I'll save it this time." She recited her number. I added it to my contacts and clicked my way through the steps to send her the pics. I sent them all. After that show of intensity, I wanted to make sure she got what she wanted.

Her phone buzzed in her purse. "Oh! Looks like I had my phone after all." She pulled it out and flipped through the images. "Perfect. Just, perfect! Oh, you look just like him. It's... uncanny. You look amazing."

I thought so. I dressed in my finest polo and my favorite jeans. I extended a hand. "Well. This is it. Thank you for everything. I guess I need to do *my part* now." I've got people to make and places to touch.

She took my hand. "Yes, right. *(Ah-hem)* Go on. And thank you again."

She watched me enter the clinic. I'm certain she didn't blink. I offered the same hand to the doc. He, too, shook it and led me to a blank, fluorescent hallway. He talked as we walked.

"Nice to meet you, Mr. Miller. I've heard much about you from Miss Livingston."

We rounded a corner. It smelled like a hospital, a nasty combination of ammonia and whatever else makes that smell. Is there a kit that hospital administrators order with ten horrible art prints and sprayable hospital smell? Probably.

"Mr. Miller, have you donated specimens before?"

"Yes, but never in a hospital setting."

The doc paused and pointed to an open exam room. "I'm not interested in any of your foul jokes, Mr. Miller." His sense of humor is clearly as colorful as his lab coat.

"I'm sorry. No, I have never donated sperm." He seemed content with that answer. He seated me in a small chair in the blank room and stood over me.

"Have you had sex or masturbated in the last seventy-two hours?" He looked at me through thick glasses. His hands paused on the clipboard.

Hmm. Tricky. What night was that? Not sex, of course, but I definitely flogged the dolphin at some point recently. "Two days ago?"

"Was it two or three days ago?"

"I'm not sure."

"Do you remember what day? Or any events surrounding the session?"

"How important is it? I mean forty-eight hours? Seventy-two? What's the difference?"

"Yes."

What the fuck kind of answer is that? "It was seventy-two hours ago." I'm lying. I don't care. I'm done with this topic. He asked me a few more questions after that. Am I sexually active outside my marriage? My last STD check? Have I ever had any ball cancers? Do I hang to the right or the left? Normal dinner conversation stuff.

After he seemed reasonably content with my answers, he left me with a cup, a few wet wipes, and a television screen. "You're welcome to browse our selection of stimulating entertainment if you need it." He smiled, checked his watch, and picked at his nostril with a fat pinky finger.

I thanked him and locked the door. I don't want anything to do with that television or the remote control that goes with it. How many other fluids have been spilled in this room? Blood, spooge, and poo-poo, too? And what about hepatitis, AIDS, and all the other diseases you normally get from having too much fun with a brunette named after a city?

I browsed some sites on my phone. Nothing raised my flag. I felt a bit like a pervert. Usually I have the decency to pull my pud in the privacy of my own home. I stopped scrolling. I swiped the internet away and opened my photo album. Alex. The photo of her, standing in the hall. This might work. I propped my phone on the desk and went to work. At a pace of about a thousand dollars per pull, I finished. Easiest sixty grand I'd ever made.

I opened the door and called to the doc. From afar, he asked, "Do you need me to come over there?" I told him it was too late. I already did. Another one lost on the doc. He collected my fruit's smoothie and escorted me to the front counter. I signed a release and was on my way.

CHAPTER S16TEEN

He snored with one arm stretched across the bed and one leg falling off completely. I heave myself from beneath his heavy, hairy arm. He'd been drinking since early afternoon so he isn't going anywhere.

I twisted on a white robe, tying it around my waist. It's cool against my skin, a friendly feeling versus the sweaty carcass of the man that lay in my bed. My husband. Those words sound gross, disturbing even. I enter the code on room 9 and peek once more at Francis to make sure he is asleep.

The man told me it's strong enough to stop a charging bull. He called it Compound X. I'm sure it has a more scientific name, but Compound X raised its price tag to five thousand dollars per liquid ounce. It's a fast drug — dissipates in minutes, not days. He called it a half-life miracle. It leaves the body too quickly to track.

I stick the needle into the tiny vial, extracting no more than a bottle cap of fluid. I look at the screen again, to make sure he is still sleeping. I have cameras in every corner of my apartment. The bedroom camera, however, is hidden in the lamp. He hadn't moved. *Thank you, Francis. Now I need you to do something for me.*

I quietly close the door to room 9. It shuts with a hushed click. The bedroom reeks of alcohol and sweat, the culmination of overindulgence and ignorant vigor. Who is this man? This, this, this, New Yorker who I'm married to. Never did he ask about me. Never! Not once! Never, never, never! He was so mesmerized by my crotch he forgot everything important.

The needle slid into the small webbing between his toes. My heartbeat quickens, I can feel it in my ears. Vick's cologne from room 9 lingers, I can still smell him. More butterflies in my pulse as my thumb pushes the plunger on the syringe. I arch my back as I watch the first rush of chemicals enter his body. Slowly, I drain more of the compound into his foot. I imagine it climbing through his veins, through his ankle and up into his thighs, through his groin, and into his flaccid, tiny cock. His chest is filling with Compound X. *Breathe, my love, breathe.* My legs quiver and my thighs tingle. My knees shivering, almost knocked into each other. I rest a finger on his neck, feeling gently for a pulse. He is still here. My breathing intensifies as I push the last hit of liquid into his foot.

He shakes, startling me. A sudden chuckle escapes me. "You scared me, Francis!" His eyes open for a moment and blink. His mouth gapes. "Almost there, honey. Shhhhhhh…" He erupts into a full body tremor. His heart skips and stutters. I feel my lip curling into a smile.

His eyes fade and I whisper, "Thank you, Francis, I'm one step closer." I kiss his forehead and slide my fingers over his eyelids to close them. I remember mother kissing my forehead as a child. It brings on sweet memories, a time when mother wasn't hiding in the amber of a pill bottle. She would sing to me at bedtime. She would kiss my forehead and whisper, "Twinkle twinkle little star… How I wonder what you are…"

I hummed the rest of "Twinkle Twinkle" with a smile as I pulled the needle from his foot and covered his limp, naked body with sheets. I wiped a bit of foam from his lips and kissed his forehead one last time.

"Goodnight, dear." I smiled, turned out the light, and closed the door.

CHAPTER SEVENTEEN

Things are good. Very good. I'd worked out a deal with some of the guys from the club on a ranch-style duplex on the south side and I was getting much needed time with the little man. I'd met with Alexa a while back to tell her about my family history. I was surprised — she'd done her homework. The meeting was short, and not as memorable as the others.

Kraya and I were doing all right, too. Seems guilt is a dish best served daily. I was feeling better about my decision, but for weeks after the donation I felt terrible. Funny how you overwork to improve a relationship when you feel like an asshole.

Kray had some weird things happening. She was up and down, forgetful and sleepy, sleepless and energetic. Post-baby, par for the course. She'd visited her nurse a few times and gotten the same answer: "*Just hormones. Relax, it'll get better.*" And she was right, she did get better. Usually right at the moment she fell asleep. More often than not, I'm riding in the caboose of her emotional roller coaster.

It's my favorite time of year so I do my fair share of tucking away feelings. I can ignore a lot when I'm a few eggnogs deep into a Christmas album. Twelve-ish inches of snow clog the sidewalks and twinkling red and green lights hang from every porch. Carolers and bell ringers are out in force, collecting money for some charity I'm not sure exists. I drop a quarter in the bucket from time to time because for fuck's sake, it's just a quarter, not one of those giant checks you get when you win the lottery.

Christmas music plays in our house from the moment the Thanksgiving bird is finished until the first day of the new year. No exceptions. My boy and I started opening doors on the advent calendar this week. He likes the candy and I like the tradition.

We were finishing up breakfast when my phone rang. The caller ID said, "A. Livingston." Kraya tilted her head curiously and pointed, her mouth too full of food to ask. "I've gotta take this, hun." I pulled the phone to my ear and answered, "Hello?"

"Good morning, Vick."

"Alex, good morning. What can I do for you?" I've gotta get the hell out of here before Kray overhears something. I head to my office, taking my phone and one more bite of bread.

"We should talk," she said. Her tone unreadable.

"We're talking now, aren't we?"

She laughed. "We are, yes, but we need to discuss some business. Privately."

I'm intrigued. "I'm free next week. Maybe Wednesday?" I had a lot going this week. Inspections, a few repairs, naps — the usual.

"I'm attending Preston's charity event tomorrow at six p.m. We'll talk there. Dress formally. I have some people I'd like to introduce you to."

Nick Preston's house? Nick is well known in the community. One of those guys so successful even B-list celebrities want to know him. He'd been in business since I was a wee lad and threw Christmas charity parties every year. Invite only. Exclusive. Coveted. I'm in. "I'll have to rearrange my schedule, but I can probably make it."

"Good. Pick me up at five-thirty."

Damn, she's cocky. Or is that confidence? Either way, kinda annoying. "Pick you up? From the tower?" I call it "the tower" now. Anyone who is anyone calls it that.

No response.

"Hello?" Nothing. Not a dropped call. Not a hang-up, just empty noise. Like she'd put the phone back in her pocket. "Alex?"

Still no response.

The screen showed we were still connected. Maybe a bad signal? I asked if she was there a few more times and hung up. I threw the phone back into my pocket and headed upstairs. I kicked a few toy cars and a blue ball from the stairs as I climbed. Kraya was elbow deep in applesauce because our kid made the decision to slap his food rather than eat it. I've had those days, too, buckeroo.

"Who was that?" Spousal curiosity — innocent, but prying.

"Oh, a friend from the club. May want to do some work together." I avoided using *he* or *she*. Plausible deniability. It's not dishonest if you don't lie, though I am getting sick of this friggen gray area.

"Oh good! Let me know what happens, okay?"

I told her I would.

We cleaned up breakfast, and talked about her week. She wiped the table in circles with a torn, wet napkin. On Monday she found a sale on double-smoked ham and diapers. Tuesday she returned that movie we never watched, and on Wednesday she had a great lunch with Clarissa. They talked about Clarissa's new boyfriend, a younger stud with aspirations of becoming a nurse. I nodded, said, "Uh huh," and mixed it up with, "Oh yeah?" and "Oh, I could see that."

Conversations with your spouse are like talking to a recording of yourself: A) You probably know how the story is going to end, B) It's always one sided, and C) The person on the other end is someone you love.

After the dishes were dried and Junior snuggled in his bed for a nap, I took off. I was fresh out of paint and one of the rentals had thirsty walls. I pushed the garage door button on the visor and waited for the door to open. Our garage was getting tighter as the years progressed. Coolers and billowing boxes line the walls. I should spend a day and work on this. But who has the time? I'll wait for spring.

Sunglasses? Check. Phone? Check. As I dug through the center console for my stuff, I saw an envelope buried under some coins and a toy whale. The garage door was still opening, so I took a sec to peek. An ATM receipt from yesterday morning. Withdrawal of four hundred dollars. Why did she withdraw that much? And why cash? We always use credit cards; the points are too good to pass up. I know she was looking at some things on eBay. Boom. I know! Christmas presents! *Sneaky, sneaky, Kray. Nice try.* I won't mention it though. If I do, she'll conceal it better the next time.

My tires crunched in the snow as I pulled out of the garage. I could hear a few neighbors scraping shovels against their driveway. I decide to scrap the paint shopping and opt for some Christmas shopping instead. Kid needs some socks and Kraya? Hmmm. Maybe a necklace? I never know what to buy her. Her gifts are always so thoughtful. Mine are usually just expensive.

Shopping was a breeze. In and out, like any proper male should be. Though it was short, I enjoyed my brief encounter with the mall. The same, wonderfully repetitive Christmas music in every store. Heck, I even made time to order a coffee and sit for a spell to enjoy the Christmas-people-watching extravaganza. Mothers with unruly kids. Grandparents with smiles and diapers. Teenagers with black hair, piercings, and testosterone. Six stores and a cup of black in sixty minutes. A new record.

After navigating the icy parking lot labyrinth, I headed home to wrap their presents. Kiddy presents are always the easiest to wrap. Loose cartoon gift paper and a few strands of clear tape is perfect. Kraya's presents were tougher. You know, wrap the paper tight and smooth, and use a ribbon around the box. I slapped a bow on the top where the ribbon made an *X*, and cut a *"To: /From:"* card from a scrap of leftover paper.

It took me ten minutes, per present, to wrap her gifts. It will take all of seven seconds to unwrap them. I think I'm in the wrong business. Someone is making a killing out there manufacturing single-use wrapping paper. What's it cost to manufacture? Maybe ten cents? I paid eight bucks for this glimmering, mistletoe-laden paper bullshit.

I stowed the presents under the tree and had a few cookies. 'Tis the season for frosted goodness and an extra ten pounds around the waistline. Kraya has been on a cookie-baking frenzy. I'm not convinced she is eating or sleeping, just cookies, cookies, cookies, twenty-four/seven. She's been in one of her "ups" — endless energy, fun, and motivation. I knew a crash was bound to happen any time now, but this was the best version of Kraya I'd seen in months. Apparently this still falls into the *somewhat normal behavior* range for the first few years of motherhood.

Kraya talked endlessly while slapping balls of cookie goodness onto the pan. I'd made myself comfortable in the living room, feet up in the recliner, throwing her a "Yep" and a "Uh-huh" when she needed one.

"...He kissed that other girl and she knew it! I told her she was worth more than that. No one should be dating someone who cheats! Annoying, isn't it? That she would go back to him? After all this..."

Mid-sentence, the sound of a tin pan hitting the tile echoed through the house. She'd dropped a pan of cookies. Was it a baked pan? Or a cookie dough pan? I held my breath and waited for the meltdown. Hold... hold! I gritted my teeth and squinted. When her mood is up, she's explosive.

Is that laughter? She was laughing! I carefully popped my head into the kitchen to see her sitting on the floor, laughing at the cookies.

"Everything okay in here, hun?"

She turned to me, eyes wide. "Oh, ha! Yes. *Yes*. Yes, yes, yes! Everything is wonderful!" Open palms pointed to the cookie mess.

Was that sarcasm? Hard to tell. "Are you sure you're okay? Is there anything I can do for you?" I cringed. Why did I ask such a stupid question? Inevitably she'd think up something.

"Yes! Thanks. I need two more pounds of sugar and a few more pounds of flour while you're at it. Oh, and can you grab some applesauce pouches, too, since you're going out?"

Is she really all right? No. She is not. She's wound up tighter than I'd ever seen her. Maybe she's about due for another check-in at the clinic.

More errands and an hour away from Kraya might be the hero I need to be right now.

CHAPTER E18HTEEN

Daddy's influence kept our short wedding and Francis's heart attack out of the papers. The media was morbidly excited to write about the *Livingston's short marriage ending after her husband's heart attack*. It took money, lots of money, to keep the press out. A favor I begged of Daddy.

I grieved publicly, weeping quietly whenever eyes were on me. I took a month off, something I never imagined possible. I cried at family dinners, too. My mother was a surprisingly wonderful shoulder to cry on. She listens to my stories and holds me in her frail arms. Does she still have some motherly instincts buried inside her?

At night I am calm. I am methodical. I trade black sweaters and puffy eyes for workout attire. I run miles on my treadmill, lift weights, and spend time in my tanning bed. I'm creating a beautiful world for us. Vick will fall prey to me because he is mine already.

I bought a new medical insurance package for him. In doing so, I needed to insure his wife... I *hate* that she gets that title first — his *wife*. I insured his son, too. Our son — He'll be mine, too, soon. His tiny heart will grow to love me, my smile, and my ability to love his father. Children can feel that kind of tenderness, that innate sense of loving. I used Vick's company to buy their upgraded insurance. Anyone can buy insurance for strangers with the right social security number, FEIN, and a credit card. It gave me a back door to all of their records and allowed me to request a routine blood panel. I need to know he is still safe. Had that bitch of a wife infected him with something worse than her presence?

I still follow him. I've gotten better though, more advanced. I use GPS tracking on his car and phone. I even have a chip in his son's shoes so I can keep an eye on him, too, if that floozy can't.

Everything is falling into place. Everything is perfect. Especially today. Today is different. My take in the second act of the play. I've learned from my mistakes and realize I need to make my own destiny. You can't rely on others to introduce us. This time will be different.

I pull into the grocery store parking lot, just a few cars behind him. He walks casually, dodging traffic as he heads to the sliding doors. "Be careful," I whisper as a redneck slams on his brakes to avoid Vick.

If he hurt him I'd pull his flannel-loving butt out of the truck and kill him where he stood. You got lucky today, Cleatus. I wait a full, agonizing minute before I follow him into the store. I check my hair, my nails, my eye shadow, and go inside.

I see him. Oh my God, I see him standing there casually in the fruit aisle. I can feel his skin against mine. His smile bright enough to illuminate the whole store. I smell his cologne and a rush of endorphins and fluids reach my core.

How long has it been since I've visited a public grocery store? Why do you walk among the commoners, Vick? You should be buying real food, not these overdone avocados and this poor excuse for a tomato. When we wed, you will see what it is like to have a personal shopper and what it tastes like to eat *real* food.

I walk behind him with shaking hands. I cannot cry. — *Do not cry!* This is it. I'm so close I can see his hair. Each, beautiful in their way — zigging and zagging. Do they know how lucky they are to grow there? The pit in my stomach grows deeper. Keep cool. Keep walking. My heels are loud on the dirty, faded tiles and it smells of musty fruit and retired women. What if he doesn't see me? What if all this work is for nothing?

Our eyes meet and I blush.

Shit. Shit. *Shit.* There he is. He sees me. He *saw me!* Gather your thoughts. Gather your strength; breathe, breathe, listen, hum, breathe, laugh, *don't laugh.* He sees you. That's it. Go with the plan. Stick with the plan. Drink the water, Vick.

CHAPTER NINETEEN

I woke to the sounds of sobbing. Not Kraya this time, but our little boy, whooping from his crib. I nudged Kraya, whose response was unintelligible, even a bit angry. I knew what she was saying, I took foreign language in college. It translated to, *"Fuck you, get him up yourself, I'm sleeping."* She popped open an angry eye and pulled up the covers. Translation confirmed.

I walked into his bedroom and pulled him out of bed. The floor was cold on my bare feet. I changed his diaper on the tall wooden changing table. I knew someday I'd need to screw it into the wall for safety, but not today, and not any of the previous days either. I put him in some orange pants and a miniature sweatshirt. Gosh this kid is cute. I slipped back into the bedroom, this time with my secret weapon — a smiling little kiddo. The dragon's eyes popped open for a moment, only to reveal a scowl and more unintelligible sounds.

We let her sleep. I made breakfast — the good kind of breakfast, none of that cereal and milk bullshit either. I cooked up some eggs, bacon, and sausages, and made orange juice and coffee. I even threw champagne in there to liven things up. I brought it to the side of our bed on a silver platter as a peace offering to the dragon goddess. She woke, turned, and eyed the food. She looked terrible, like a drag queen after a night of too much coke. She rolled toward us and began grazing. We sat with her while she ate. It took her about twenty minutes to come back to life after snarfing down the breakfast in bed. Whether it was the food or the champagne, she was vertical and able to look after Junior while I went out for a bit. Mission accomplished.

As I pulled on some jeans and a Rush concert t-shirt, I asked her about last night. She said, "I was just so wired. I don't know what came over me." Totally *normal*, I'm sure. I love the woman, but she's been a train wreck for a while. "I made plenty of cookies though! Feel free to take some with you today." I threw some in a baggie before I left. How could I resist?

I, on the other hand, woke up invigorated. Ready to roll. I was excited to meet *the* Nick Preston, the legend, the myth, the rich prick who owned most of the East End. I'd heard stories and seen pictures but I never thought I'd meet those Ivy League assholes in person. I was also trying to bury the idea that I was looking forward to seeing Alex.

I threw my duffel bag in my car and left the house. First stop was the gym. I spent some time on the elliptical, got my heart rate up to one-seventy, and called it good after my shirt looked like Chris Farley'd walked a few feet. I cooled down on the treadmill until I could hear the hot tub calling my name. I answered. After fifteen minutes of cooking in the tub, I took a shower. A long, cool one. I stood in the shower for ten or fifteen minutes, palms pressed against the white tile with a smile on my face. It's rare that I get to separate from my cell phone. Rare to be away from the wife and kid, too. I shaved, cleaned up my eyebrows, and trimmed my nose hairs. I cleaned all the other areas I usually neglect, too. Before I left I said hello to a few old guys I know and pulled my clothes out of my locker.

Next, I picked up my dry cleaning. It was "Trenty-a-dorrars" for a couple shirts and pants. After that I caught some lunch. I grabbed a turkey Italian hoagie from Dominick's Deli on 29th Avenue. I'm here once a week, so I qualify as a regular. I could smell burnt coffee, mustard, and a hint of bacon when I walked in. The store windows were tinted, but had decades of scratches in the film letting in white lasers of light every few feet. As usual, the owner was standing behind the long glass case of meats, cheeses, and various colors of vegetables, watching soccer on an old tube TV hanging on the far wall.

This guy was a character, a gem. Not necessarily a nice guy, but a fun one to watch. He ever so delicately sliced the salami and pepperoni like he was performing open heart surgery. He laid them on the bread carefully, and maintained the balance of greens to meat perfectly. Then, he sprayed spicy mustard and oil haphazardly across the top of the sandwich like an overpowered fire hose. Careful setup, clumsy ending. He always makes sandwiches like that.

I ate my sandwich in the deli. No other customers entered, none left. I was all alone with my thoughts and my red and white checkered tablecloth for twenty minutes before my phone buzzed. I wiped a few crumbs from the screen and read the text from Kraya: "My fucking hair is falling out!" Accompanied with the text was a picture. It was a shot of her hand, with the bathroom floor in the background. A big chunk of hair lay flat in her palm.

Awesome. This is exactly what I needed today. I texted back: "Oh no! How? What?" Am I concerned? Yeah, I am, but these freakish occurrences were a pretty common addition to our family.

"In the shower. Just now. They just… fell out! I was washing my hair and a few clumps just fell out! Ugh! I look terrible!"

"Take a picture, let me see where it came from." I picture Britney Spears after her meltdown.

"I'll show you when you get home!" Accompanied by a long string of frownie faces.

"Very sorry that's happening to you, babe! I'll be home in a bit and I'll take a look."

"Can't you come home now? I'm worried. I read online that it might be allergies. I threw away all of our soap and shampoo. Can you pick up new shampoo and conditioner on your way home?"

"I have *no* idea what to get you for shampoo and conditioner." Seriously, have you seen those aisles at the store? There are too many options. Moisturizing, curling, dry-scalp, oily-scalp, passion fruit, unscented, straightening...

"Just pick one."

"Really?"

"Really."

"I'll be home in a bit. Don't forget I have that party tonight." I wait. No response.

That could mean a few things. One, she is annoyed that I'm thinking about the party while she is having a hair loss meltdown — or — two, something else happened, hair or general kid-related issues.

I picked up some shampoo, soap, and conditioner that the lady said was "good for sensitive skin." It's probably safe to assume her skin is sensitive if it's shedding its own hair, right? When I got home, I was surprised. Not because of her hair, that looked okay. (Just okay; there were a few patches missing but nothing a quick comb-over couldn't hide). I was surprised because she was lying on the floor in the kitchen, chuckling to herself, listening to loud music — drunk.

"What the *fuck*, Kray!?"

CHAP2ER TW20TY

After the supermarket, I cried like a little girl. No, no, not sadness. The kind of giggling tears that happen after you kiss your first boy. I buried my face in my hands in room 9, laughing. I cried, chuckled, laughed, and cried. It was so sweet, so successful. It couldn't have gone better.

I'm so proud of myself for keeping it together. I stuck to the plan. I wanted to scream and jump into his arms. I wanted to feel his hands on my back, his breath on my neck, and the warmth of his lips against mine. I wanted him. No, no, I *needed* him. But the plan was perfect. I can't stop now, I can't slow my campaign. Balls are rolling now that cannot be unrolled.

I looked at the bottle of vanilla on the table, standing in glory because the hands of an angel held it. Touched by a god no more than 25 minutes ago. A *god!* I can hardly touch it. I could feel him on the label. Sense his pheromones. His every fiber was so close I could taste him. His DNA is fresh here.

I dared to touch it. Tingles raced down my arms as I inch closer to the bottle of vanilla. I snatch it, like a devious child stealing a roll of candy. I rub it with my thumb. He. Is. Perfection.

I stopped visiting his house every night because I have better control now. I make entry only when needed — when the plan calls for action. Like tonight, Kraya's cocktail of medication needs to be changed. She is adjusting to the drugs and she has become almost functional. Like mother and *her* drugs.

I've created a perfect blend of uppers and downers. Oxycodone to put her to sleep and ephedra to bring her up. Sometimes, I mix some Adderall into the mix to see how she handles it.

I rigged more cameras around their house. I added some in his car and others in hers. I can hear more with advanced microphones, enough to know when someone is dreaming lightly or smacking their lips. I watch from my phone, from the living room, from board meetings on a tablet, from room 9. I watch them everywhere.

My most recent triumph came when I gave her a particularly heavy dose. Kraya fell asleep in less than 10 minutes, a new record. I entered through the back door, as usual. I found her macaroni in a pan on the counter. I put the pan back on the stove and cranked up the heat to high. I checked on her in the bedroom, too.

She was sleeping soundly, snoring into a big patterned pillowcase. His son was crying, so I held him. I whispered calm songs in his ear. But he didn't calm down. He cried harder and wriggled and sobbed. Someday soon, love, someday soon you'll be with Vick and me and know I am your new mother. I'll care for you and give you and your father everything, everything you want, and everything you need will be yours. I whisper in his ear, loud enough to get past his obnoxious wailing, "Your mother is a peasant cunt. You'll realize that soon." I received a notification on my phone that Vick was moving. He was coming home. He is coming *here*. It took painful energy to leave, knowing he would be here soon, in this very spot. I could meet him again. Hug him *here!* We could make love in his house, in his bed. It would be beautiful.

I put "our son" down and slipped back downstairs. I put my heels on and snuck out the sliding door. I got into my car and left, holding my phone with one hand and the steering wheel with the other. I waited and watched. I spied as he lost his cool, throwing the pan into the sink. I watched as he lost faith in his wife. I watched him save his son from the smoke.

Your time is short, Kraya.

I will win.

CHAPTER TWENTY-ONE

Kraya lay on the floor, eating potato chips. "I... I... only had one glass of (hiccup) wine. So shoot me!" Patches of her hair were scattered around her. "Oh, and don't worry — he's fine. He's upstairs." She lifted the video baby monitor, showing an image of him sleeping soundly in his crib.

I breathed a sigh of relief. "Your hair? Is it still..."

"Falling out?" She pulled out another bunch, looking at it with a squinted, glazed eye. "I made an appointment with the doc tomorrow."

Kneeling, I grabbed her by the shoulders, squaring my body to hers. "Kray, honey. I'm so sorry about your hair. But you're drunk. Our kid is upstairs. What if something happened?"

"Something *did* happen, Vick." With arms crossed, she continued, "Asshole. Don't you remember?" She pointed to the piles of hair around her.

I need to be at the tower in a few hours. This can't be happening. "Yes, I remember, but right now I need to make sure someone is caring for our child. You're drunk..."

She interrupted. "I'm *buzzed*. And I *told* you, I only had one glass of wine. You don't believe me!"

There is a time to choose your words carefully. This wasn't one of those times. "No. I don't believe you, Kray, you're wasted! I know you had a bad day, and it sucks that your hair is acting weird, but you're a mom. You need to make sure our..."

"I'm *not* wasted. Buzzzzzzzzzzzed..." She tried to get to her feet, instead she lay back down. "I'm only buzzed. And he's fine. He's been sleeping for a while."

"What happens when he wakes up from his nap?"

"I was going to get him! He's so cute, isn't he?"

"Seriously? I'm so very done with this conversation. I'm calling Molly. I can't do this, not tonight."

Sad. Pissed. Worried. Annoyed? I couldn't quite peg which one I am most. A fucked-up cluster of emotions, I guess. I called Molly, our neighbor, who does some freelance babysitting.

She was nineteen, overweight, and responsible. Her night was booked, but not too busy to turn down a hundred bucks. I tucked in Kraya, fed the munchkin, and put on my best shirt. It was obnoxiously convenient that Kraya was sleeping. I'll avoid a lot of questions about the night when I get home.

I slipped on a pair of pressed pants, a sharp belt, polished shoes, and then threw a blazer over my shoulder and waited. Molly was twenty minutes late, leaving a crappy, short window for me to make my scheduled pickup at five-thirty. I'm still pissed at Kray, but I can't spend energy on that right now. There are people in high places looking to swing some deals tonight and I'm going to be one of them, dammit.

I looked in the mirror and realized my suit looked pretty darn good. Not millionaire sharp, but I looked like a guy who knew how to dress. Fancy watch, mirrored shoes, and a suit jacket that fit just right. I checked the time. *Shit.* I said my goodbyes, kissed the kid, and ran out the door.

I pulled up to the tower between the valet stand and the decorative main entrance. Late, but here. I flipped the radio station from Christmas music to the news. I couldn't begin to guess what music she listened to.

Five minutes passed. Then ten. Finally fifteen minutes. I called her. On the first ring, I spotted her heading toward my car. I hung up and completely forgot about my grievance with her tardiness. I forgot about everything. She was breathtaking in her gown. An elegant, red number that framed her body tighter than plastic wrap on a pallet. A white fur scarf rounded her shoulders, protecting her from the winter air. Not too scandalous, not too conservative, but a perfect combination of sophistication and beauty. Here we go again.

I remind myself that I'm married by looking at my ringed hand on the steering wheel. *I have a kid. I'm happily married.* You know, all those things you forget when a perfect piece of tail smiles at you. She paused outside the car door, peeking in.

CHAPTER 2WENTY-2WO

I've been waiting all night for him to call. I sit in room 9, eyes trained on my silent cell phone. The room is stale with the smell of rubber and sweat and raspberry lotion. The eBay jacket I bought from him hangs loosely around my shoulders, and I clench the bottle of vanilla tightly. It's been a long, sleepless night. I can't tell what time it is. Is it past dinner? Coming up on breakfast? I set my water on the desk next to 6 empty water bottles.

Will he test his marriage for me? Is he learning the truth now, about his own feelings? About himself? He knows he loves me. He knows his heart burns and lusts for my attention.

While I wait, I rub the bump of skin just above my lips. My phone rings, buzzing along the table against the stillness of the night. I fear a stroke — my pulse rockets beyond a healthy range. I slap myself hard enough to snap back into reality, but soft enough not to damage the years of work I'd put into my skin. Years I've sacrificed for him. *To be perfect.* For *this* chance.

I clear my throat and smile.

"Professor. I knew you'd call." Was that over the top? Too thick? I need to keep it professional. Keep it tight. Stick with the plan.

"Oh, wait, is this Pizza Palace?" Vick said.

Funny. He is *so* funny. Did he come up with that on the spot? *God, he's funny!* It took me a second to contain myself. Be sensible, Alexa, be professional.

"You've had time to review my offer. I hope you're calling to say yes."

He paused there, breathing into the microphone. I listened so intensely I could probably hear *his* heartbeat if I focused. My hand shook as I pressed the phone to the side of my head. Harder and harder I pressed, hoping if I can get the speaker a bit closer, I'd be that much closer to him — that much closer to his lips. I thought of hanging up, dialing 9-1-1 — my heart can't sustain this stress. My chest hurts. Speak! *Are you going to take it?* I'm going to die. I'm going to die right now. My heart is going to start sputtering and I'm going to fall to the floor. It'll be days before they find me in here.

"I appreciate your offer. I'd be more interested if it said 60,000 dollars. If you'll adjust your contract, I'll reconsider."

More money? *More money*? That is the only barrier? I've got him. I've got you, my clam, my rock, my little pony. You do love me. He's learning to play the game. He can't just run to me, he needs to take it slow and let Kraya down easy. What a gentleman. But, c'mon, Vick. Just 60,000 dollars? Oh, sweetheart, you need to learn how to read your opponent. We'll work on that together, you and me. I would have taken 200,000 dollars. Maybe half a million? Ugh... for you, any number.

Pulsing red drumbeats cloud my vision. Calm down, Alexa. *Calm down*. Play it by the book. Drink the water. I cleared my head and spoke. "You're feistier than I expected, Professor." Good. Great! Keep it cool. Keep it casual. Have fun with him for Christ's sake.

"Vick, Miss Livingston. Just Vick."

Oh God! Oh! Vick! You're really you! We're really doing this, aren't we! Play nice and play back... "Just Vick." I'm in hysterics. I put the phone on mute for a moment to catch my breath. Pause, honey, pause. Take your time. I click the *unmute* button — "I'll accept your offer for 60,000 dollars and sweeten the pot by offering a 5-year membership to the Orchard Path Golf Club. But this offer is only good right now. Are you going to make me a happy woman? Or disappoint me?"

Too much. I gave him too much! He's playing me now. Happy? Disappoint? The golf club? Father will kill me for that. I don't care. Oh, I don't *care!* The willows and the earth rejoice together, I don't care! I want to see him. I want to touch him. I want him to be so happy he runs to me, begging for more, begging for me with tears in his eyes!

"As for the disappointment or happiness, that's between you and your shrink..." He laughed a beautiful laugh. "But I'll sign." He is *so funny! Ahhhhh!* His laugh is so genuine and humor so quick. What a funny, funny man. I love his wit! And he said *yes! Yes!* Oh fuck yes, Vick! We're doing it! But he is right, I *do* need to call my shrink sometime. He is always right.

"Yes? Yes! Great! Yes! Wonderful! The instructions are on the packet. I'll have a new draft written with the new dollar amount. Can you still make it on time?" *I can't believe it!* It's working!

"My attorney still has the contract. Can you give me the details again?"

"Of course! You'll need to go to The Twelfth Floor Clinic in our building." I continued to tell him about the appointment. Am I rambling? It doesn't matter! He loves me. I can feel it. True love doesn't care if you babble happily. A few more pieces to the puzzle and we can finally be together.

"You're going to give me something I've wanted for a long, long time, Vick. Thank you. See you in a bit."

He hung up and I hung up. I pulled the vanilla bottle out with a pop and set it back on its shrine.

"Much to do. Much to do!" I sing it. I can't believe I'm singing.

I picked up the newest photoshopped pictures of Vick from the printer. Room 9 is already covered, wall to wall, with pictures of Vick. I'd even added myself to many of the photos. Kissing him. Hugging him. Laughing with him. It didn't take much to crop out and replace that hussy.

This new batch of pictures was different. These were edited with care taken in the details. After 3 online classes and 14 hours on YouTube, I learned how to photoshop any image to perfection.

With practice, weeks upon weeks of practice, I'd learned how to add moles and freckles. I could adjust his hair color, too. I feel guilty, like I am changing the paint on the Mona Lisa or altering the Sistine Chapel.

Stick with the plan, Alexa. Stay with me.

I hang the new pictures around my apartment and kiss the glass over his cheek.

CHAPTER TWENTY-THREE

My tires chomped through the snow until they came to a stop on the circle driveway. I opened her car door when we arrived. She grabbed my hand to steady herself on the icy drive. Such a gentle grip. Dainty and sweaty. Gross, but tolerable considering the rest of the body it's attached to. Pools of red fabric lingered along her body. Focus, chump. I'm here for business.

"I didn't know you were a gentleman, too, Vick. We should do this more often," she said and winked with a jovial smile.

Woman, please. Are you flirting with me? Or are you joking because we are only here because you need something from me? Is this the way you are with everyone?

Whatever. I'm just going to keep doing my thing — meeting, greeting, and schmoozing. Hopefully, I'll score some great contacts from this thing. My "date" isn't bad to look at, but she is just eye candy and a pocketbook.

The driveway was brick, surrounded by snow-covered shrubs, real red brick, not those stamped concrete fakers. Preston's house is massive. A house that makes you wonder what his mortgage payment must be. Ten thousand? Eight K? Twenty? That roofline, too, incredible! Windows and jutting eaves on every surface. The snow-covered roof must cost a fortune to re-shingle.

A few ogres stood next to the mansion entrance. Earpieces, parkas, and peeking guns at their waists. I took a stab that they weren't the cooks.

Alexa and her high heels navigated the bricks with unsteadiness solved by gripping my hand. It was the most attention I'd received in longer than I can remember.

I felt a bit dirty, like I was cheating. Had anyone ever gotten a divorce for holding another woman's hand? Doubtful. But that's a pretty shitty measure of right and wrong. Didn't matter anyhow. She released her grip once we reached flat land. Nothing to it. No need to overanalyze.

Alexa showed the burly security guards her invitation, a chocolate factory golden ticket looking thing. He lifted his sunglasses to inspect it. Creases along his brow told me he'd seen plenty. Those wrinkles aren't made by sipping lattes by the water cooler; he'd been places and taken some punches. I'll stay out of his way.

The inside of the home was nothing as I'd imagined. I had images of contemporary steel beams and vast glass railings, a house so modern it looked dangerous. But this was nothing like that. Nick Preston had a taste for the north woods. The cabin life. And he didn't mind paying for it.

The vaulted ceilings extended three of four stories. Everything was wood — knotty, glossy pine like you'd see in a lake home. It's done well though, not like the cabin you visited when you were seven. This place has every feature of a mansion, mixed with the comfort of a woodland retreat. The entrance boasted lavish, marble tables for gifts and a butler to take your coat. Shit. I didn't even consider a gift. Next time. Next time? Ha! I like that.

The butler, a tan, mid-sixties gentleman by the name of Dirk took Alex's white fur from her shoulders. She mouthed a pleasant thank-you.

"What do you think, Vick?"

"It's nice. I've always wanted to come to Preston's Christmas party." We walked into the main hall. We'd passed a grand staircase and another set of side rooms, all adorned with cocktail dresses, tuxedos, and rich pricks.

"I'm glad you could come on such short notice, Professor." She held up a manicured hand to her lips. "Oops, not professor. Vick." A polite smile grew. "It is a good opportunity for you to meet more people in the industry. I like helping you, Vick."

A few women passed, drinking eggnog and gossiping. You know you're mingling with an eccentric crowd when you overhear the words *nanny* and *cashmere* in the same sentence.

"Thank you. I appreciate the invitation. It's an amazing opportunity." I notice the Christmas music isn't being played over the stereo. A skeletonized woman in an adjacent room is playing the piano while "Jingle Bells" is being sung by a group of drunken businessmen, crowded happily around her piano.

"I can't get over it. I'm not sure if I ever will! It's amazing. You're a dead ringer for my Francis. If I didn't know better, I'd think you were him." She cocked her head, eyeing me like a T-bone. "It feels good to be with him again, and to have him as a date to a party. You're quite amazing, Vick. Thank you for helping me."

"Champagne?" a Hispanic waitress interrupted.

Thank God she showed up. I didn't want Alex sliding into another crying session. I make it a habit not to make my dates cry until at least the third date. And I could really use the booze. "Yes, please, I'll take one." But she isn't a date, dude, remember, this is business.

She passed me a napkin-crusted champagne glass, bubbling with golden courage. I sipped it and looked at Alex. She'd made eye contact with a portly gentleman in an ill-fitting suit. He parted the crowd and approached with a kind wave. "Alexa Livingston! My goodness! It's been ages! How is your father?" Awkward fella. His jacket had cocktail sauce down the face and his comb-over was a mess. He had a jovial, rosy-cheeked smile and a deep laugh that complemented him well.

She hugged him. "Father is good! Thank you. Marie? Tell me she is well now?" She sipped from her champagne flute.

"My, what a good memory!" He turned to me, nudging me with an elbow "Better not do anything wrong, she'll remember forever!"

Does he think we are together? Does everyone else think it, too?

"Marie is fine. Nothing the docs couldn't fix. She got out about six weeks ago. You can't stop her. She's already back in Italy doing what she does best!"

They both laughed. I hate these situations. I want to laugh, too, but I have no idea what they're talking about. Alex touched my shoulder.

"I'm sorry, I didn't introduce you. Victor, this is Lawrence. Lawrence Carmichael."

He stretched a full set of sausage fingers in my direction.

"Nice to meet you, Lawrence." I shifted my champagne from my right hand to my left and shook his hand. His hands aren't strong, but not weak either. I could tell he'd shaken a lot of hands through the years. A smile accompanied the handshake with polite vigor.

He cupped his other hand on mine, moving closer to me with personal flair. "Nice to meetcha, Victor. Don't let this one get you in too much trouble!" He turned and winked at Alexa.

She nudged his arm. "He's the one who will get you in trouble." They both laughed and Sausage Fingers released his grip.

I wonder if that is a cliché. Do they know each other well? Do they really enjoy one another? I've heard some variation of this exact conversation a thousand times in polite company. It's a dance. A dance that plays out in a series of trained steps. Always the same, different dance partners. Always light-hearted, good-natured banter that ends with a quip. As unauthentic as it comes, yet everyone continues.

"It's good to see you, Lawrence. I'm sorry, but I need to introduce Victor to a few other people." They exchanged a few more *good to see you's* and Alex washed him away.

"Vick..." She pointed. "There he is. Nick Preston." A fit, older man with blond, windswept hair and an untied tie stood next to the bar. I assume the flirtatious twenty-something girl with the boob job and the short dress is his wife. "I'll introduce you."

CH4PTER 2WENTY-4OUR

Is he watching me? Does he have cameras in my apartment, too? Does he watch me watch him, wondering when the day will come that he finally reveals himself? I'll find out someday. Today though, I need to focus. I need to stay on task. Stick with the plan.

I'm slipping her stronger drugs. Higher highs and lower lows. It's become quite a fun show to watch. Beauty and the peasant. I should trademark that — a cartoon about a beautiful man who marries a demented, slutty peasant who slipped in under my nose to marry him. Cunt. *Cunt!*

He is here now. I see his car in the parking lot security cameras. He carries himself with such dignity. Is there anything he can't do well?

I'm getting nervous. Is my dress too short? Too long? Am I beautiful enough to catch his attention for even a moment? Have I been trying hard enough? Okay, okay, slow down. Let's go through this. Did you work out today? Check. Lotion three times an hour? Check. I even bought a four thousand dollar bottle of Mag' Metera, a French lotion. All the girls at the tennis club rave about it. Makeup? Check. But is it the right shade? Do my lips look too glossy? Too pink?

My phone buzzes. It's Daddy. "Where are we on the Nurbaker estate?"

Too much stress. Are you kidding? Vick is walking into the building right now. Daddy, *not now!* Is my makeup right? "Fuck!" My scream echoes in the empty apartment. I slam my fist into the table, knocking over containers of lip gloss, eyeliner, and perfume. A lipstick case rolls from the makeup table to the floor.

Stick with the plan. Trust me. Trust the plan. I nod to myself. "Yes. I can do this." I stand and go to the front door, open it, walk out, and push the elevator *call* button.

My elevator arrives immediately. I'm fidgeting. Am I ready? Are my heels the right height? Lips? Skin? Is the contract ready? *"Stop. Just stop!"* My voice echoes in the small elevator. The numbers descend on the small screen. Floor 15. Then 12. Soon 5 and then a ding. My heart, oh my poor heart. Can it take this stress?

I need to hurry now. As I wind through the building I can hear him. The voice of a god, gracing us with his presence in my own building. I round the corner to the lobby.

"I have an appointment with…"

He looks… just wow! So handsome and genuine, truly a sight to behold. He was speaking to the receptionist. She better not flirt. *You better not flirt, bitch*, I swear. I swear I will fire you faster than you can say *Livingston!*

"Me."

I found my confidence. Here I am, Vick. I've worked hard for this. I know why you're here. I'm controlling everything today, Vick. I'm bringing you here to finally realize who you love. Me. Me. Me. I know you, Vick. I know you…

The receptionists didn't look at me. Good. Peasants shouldn't look at him either. I must retire to my quarters with Vick. Ah, that sounds lovely.

"C'mon, Vick." I waved for him to follow. I can't believe my Vick is following me. He is so close I can feel him. What, 2 feet away? This is incredible. Surreal. Is he looking at my hair? I think I straightened the back. Right? Did I straighten it? Fuck, fuck, fuck, it's a rat's nest, I know it. It's terrible. He is back there thinking about how dreadful my hair is.

Stop. *Stop!* He is here for you, *Alex*. To see you. He knows the plan. He is *in on* the plan. Relax. He is here to make beautiful things happen. My shoulders drop. I'm right, I need to relax; he is here for me. I turn and smile to Vick. He smiles back.

I pressed the *call* button for the elevator. He stands with the confidence of a prizefighter. I could smell him. Not his cologne, his skin. That natural scent he is releasing. Vick! We're here! Let's profess our love and stop this silly game! No. No! The plan is the only way. The way we both need to take to make sure our relationship is natural and long and real and beautiful. Our relationship will be stronger than ever. Take the water, Vick.

I press the code on the elevator, 1130. The time he was born. He acts like he didn't see the passcode, but he did and he knows exactly what it is. This is getting fun now, the hoops we must leap through to be together. The path we must walk.

"We'll need to stop at my apartment first. My lawyers drafted a new copy and should have it finished and waiting." I hear myself talking again like I'm on autopilot. Thank God for the plan. I've recited this two hundred times in the mirror. Practice makes perfect.

CHAPTER TWENTY-FIVE

"Nice to meet you, Vincent." Nick Preston threw a handful of cashews into his mouth and shook my hand.

"Victor. Not Vincent." I squeezed his hand.

"Ah, I'm sorry." He shook his head, smacking his forehead with an open palm. "*Victor.* Nice to meet you. Miss Livingston tells me you're quite a commercial real estate investor."

"Residential. I'm not sure I would qualify as…"

Alexa swatted playfully at my belly. "Stop being modest, Vick," she said and invaded my space. Nick's, too. She leaned between us, touching both of our shoulders, "He has plenty of properties around town. We've used his expertise many times. Isn't that right, Vick?"

Her eyes pierced me as if to say *don't fuck this up, kid.* I'd never been asked anything by Livingston Properties. Except, of course, to drop my kids off in a Dixie cup. She wants me to lie and gain credibility with Nick Preston by slipping him a white untruth.

In life, when someone is presented with a surefire opportunity to get ahead, but it requires a bit of dishonesty, I lean on one simple rule: *Twist the truth and flatter. Always together, separate when you're caught.*

"Yeah, we've dabbled, but nothing compared to your successes, Mr. Preston." I grab a handful of cashews, lob them into my mouth, and swig the remainder of my champagne when I'm done chewing.

"Good, good. I have a few friends in the same business. I'll have them reach out." He smiled and nodded approvingly. "Always opportunities, never enough good people to help seize them." His wife (or girlfriend?) slid her hand around his neck, kissing his cheek. "Ah. Bell. Just in time to meet Victor and Alexa Livingston." Bell — cute name, but is it a nickname or her real name? Errr, stripper name? Was she a dancer he'd plucked out and groomed for high society?

"Hi, Victor. Nice to meet you." She feigned a curtsy. "Handsome man you have there, Alexa."

Definitely a stripper. Or a college kid with great stems.

"Can you check the water in the hot tub, Bell?" She left and I watched. A magical ass on that one. Matter of fact, most of the women around there were pretty decent. Alexa and "Bell" were (by far) the frontrunners, but there were some great pieces of tail wandering about. Aside, of course, from the rich old cougars preying on the bartenders and nephews of the barons. I grabbed another much-needed drink from the top of the champagne pyramid.

Nick lowered his voice. "Excuse my wife. She's young. Great gal, but doesn't have much of a filter." I sipped my champagne, then chugged. He mentioned a few more hushed comments about her. Something about a pre-nup and her new horses. I am far more concerned with my need for alcohol than his issues with li'l Mrs. Sunshine.

"He is handsome though. She has a point." Alexa pinched my cheek like I was a four-year-old. Sometimes I feel like a tool. A mirror of a husband she once knew, important only for my DNA. Other times I think — whatever the fuck ever — as long as she keeps making it rain.

A laughing duo of oligarchs chimed in from out of nowhere. "He does look familiar, doesn't he?" the mustached one said with a grin.

"Cousin Nathaniel, perhaps?" the thinner one asked.

"No, no. Someone else." Mustachio eyed me, trying to peg the resemblance.

Alexa covered her mouth with an open palm. She excused herself and walked away swiftly, disappearing into the crowd.

"Was is something we said?"

CHAPTER 2WENTY-6IX

"Oh, yeah. No problem," Vick said and looked at his reflection in the mirrored elevator walls.

He *wants* to come into my apartment. He is hoping you'd invite him in. Good boy, Vick.

"Good. Thank you." I pause, pulling my skirt to a lower length. *Stop fidgeting.* "Nice day out there." It's not a nice day. It's cold. Freezing. What are you thinking?

"Could be better, could be worse."

I'd pay him a million dollars right now, to get a glimpse into his mind. To suck the thoughts out of his head and print them on a sign.

"Long drive to the office, ah?" he said and laughed. "You're apartment is one floor up — that's wild."

"It's quite nice. But it can feel a bit isolated. I can spend weeks, sometimes months inside this tower. Easy to forget the outside world." It *is* lonely. Lonely without you, Vick. I want you here, with me, in my apartment forever — you will love it here. Soon you'll be living with me and you'll be happy here. Please take the water.

We exit the elevator and walked to my front door. I enter the time of his birth again, a subtle reminder I know everything about him.

He entered, embracing the sights of his future home. He looks at the closed door to room 9 and watched it for a moment. Does he know about this room? Does he know I dedicate this shrine to him? Certainly he does if he is watching me. If not, I'll tell him on our honeymoon. It will be my wedding gift to him, my collection of his collection. His life in videos, clothing, smells, and touches.

I open my mouth to say, *Take off your pants, honey. I want to feel you inside me. I want your body in mine. Your hands in mine. Mine. You're mine. I want you to feel good here. With me.* But I don't say it. I need to stick with the plan — you've rehearsed this. Speak with confidence. Speak with intent.

"This is it! Cozy, but I love it."

We continue the tour, traveling through a few rooms and into my office. I'm proud of my photoshopping skills. I caught him looking at pictures of his alter ego on the walls. He smirked at a few of the pictures.

"Shit, it's not here yet." I pull open an email to Gordon but check over my shoulder first. He can't see the screen, so I write, *"Gordon, please send me the contract now. I'm ready for it."* I'd told him earlier not to send it to me until I sent him an email. He did exactly as told. Good Gordon. Good boy.

"I pay them enough, you'd think they could send things on time." Can he tell I'm not really annoyed? This was tough when I rehearsed it, feigning madness in my bedroom acting class. "I'm sorry, it'll be a few more minutes. Can I show you around while we wait?" I watched him. Did his eye twitch? Is he okay? Does he even want to see the rest of the place? Can I show you room 9, *please*?

He shrugged and we began the tour. Take the water.

We started in the kitchen. Here it is, step 148. "Vick…" I open the refrigerator. The fourth water bottle from the left is his; prepared specially for him in the late hours of the night.

The practice of putting small amounts of ecstasy in someone's system without their knowledge is called micro dosing. It increases the activity in their pleasure centers and makes them happier. If you dose someone every time you see them, they start to associate you with pleasure. Sex. Love. Peace. Everything I feel when I see him. Pavlov would be proud of me.

"Would you like a water?" This is it. *Take it. Take it.* Take the water!

"Sure."

I hand him the bottle. His fingertips grip the sides while his other hand twists the top. He lifts. Lifts higher. Higher. As the water bottle touches his lips, his eyes transfer to mine, watching me as he drinks the cold liquid. He blinks and drinks and his endorphins start to shimmy and dance. His heart rate increases, and his eyes dilate. None of which is perceivable if the dose is right. He feels calmer, cooler, and sexier.

I need to kill some time, but only a few minutes for this to fully kick in. I place my hand on the countertops and give him some spiel about the granite. I watch his eyes. Are they glossier? Is his smile stronger? Did he wink at me? No. Couldn't be. He sipped the water again.

We tour a few more rooms. Does he understand that I'm clean, unlike his wife — that clutter-hoarding whore? I watch her dig through drawers and leave dishes scattered about. An animal she is. Filthy and unkempt. I make an excuse for the mess, knowing full well my apartment is pristine compared to the junkyard his wife makes him live in.

He points to the cameras. "What's up with the eye in the sky?" He knows. He must. Is this a joke? Is he baiting me? Nice move, Vick. Gosh, I love you! Play the game, Alex, play the game.

"My husband and I liked to travel. We had them installed to watch the dogs while we were away." He shrugged. I can't tell what he's thinking.

I lure him into the bedroom. The final stop in our journey. Not today though, Vick. Today we will not make love here. Another time we will make love on this bed, right here, but not today. Unless, of course, you want to? Do you want to? Can I take you? Now? Here? In this bed, between the sheets with our bodies laced together with warmth and sweat?

I'm dizzy. Vick — my professor of love is standing here, in my room, looking at me, so close he could touch my bed. My heart beats faster. I feel a light glow of perspiration along my brow, between my legs, and on my chest. I'm sweating, *fuck*, I'm sweating. Gross! You've got to calm down. This is the moment you've wanted.

Get it together. *Stop fidgeting. Stop fidgeting.* Is your hair a mess? Dress too short? Lips the right color? Am I losing it? I'm losing it. The world is getting darker. I'm going to pass out. Shit, shit, *shit,* I'm going to pass out. This is embarrassing! Ugh, stop. Stop! *Stop!*

My phone buzzes. It's Gordon. It reads: "Contract is ready. See attached. Sincerely, Gordon McKay, ESQ, Attorney at law, Livingston Property, Inc."

I snap out of it just before the lights go out. I feel less weight on my knees. "Ah, the contract is here." I think I'm going to be okay... for now, anyhow.

CHAPTER TWENTY-SEVEN

I caught up to Alex in one of the pool rooms. This room, another abnormally tall, ridiculously built space, was peppered with bear and moose heads from hunting trips. It was deserted, with the exception of a few wrinkled, drunken duchesses sitting in the hot tub.

"You okay?" She was drinking. Not champagne — no, she'd graduated into something stronger and darker. Smelled of whiskey and chlorine from the pool.

"Yes, I'm sorry for leaving you out there." She sipped again, finishing the tumbler. She let out one of those "wow" sounds at the end of the long sip, short for, *"Dang, that's strong stuff."*

"No, it's all right. You looked like you needed a moment." As the words left my lips, she cried. A silent, mouth open cry that lasted too long. She hugged me. Hard. If I knew she was going to break down, I would have given her another ten minutes. I lifted my arms, thought for a moment, and then committed to the hug. *Shit.*

This may be the best time to ask her why, why am I here tonight? What do you want? If there is anything I can give her, now is the time. Anything to help her stop this horrid stream of wetness that is drizzling down the front of my shirt.

"Alex..." I hugged her. "Name it. What can I do for you?" She peeled her face from my chest with a sniffle.

"Yes. There is, Vick." She pawed at the strips of running mascara. "It didn't work." More waterworks. "I'm not pregnant..." She hugged me tighter.

Okay. Think about this, buddy. What now? Choose your words carefully. You knew you weren't here because she likes you; she needs more you-juice and now is the time to give it to her, but at a steep price. Negotiating with a fragile woman may seem harsh, but I've got bills to pay. "Do you need another sample?"

She lifted her head, still clinging to me. "I do... but it needs to be different." She shook her head. "I can't believe I'm asking you this. I'm *so* embarrassed."

"No, no. Go ahead. You're not embarrassing yourself! I'm the guy who had to jack off in a cup, remember?" Too far. Dangit. Was that too redneck for her? She smiled. Maybe it was just the right amount of blue collar humor she needed.

She lets go of a quick laugh and nods her head. "Yes, I need it again. Two samples this time, twenty-four hours apart…"

"Easy. I can do that." Stop crying. Please stop crying! Oh, and I'll need money, too, lady. We can discuss that once you put your face back on.

Her smile returns, but not completely. I can tell she is holding something back. "The rest… is…" she stuttered, "complicated."

"How is this complicated?"

"We need to be in the same room. I need a…" She made air quotes and changed her voice to sound like a man. "…fresher specimen. Immediately after ejaculation it needs to be inserted."

Immediately after ejaculation, it needs to be inserted. I paused and thought about that sentence. Never have I heard such a personal, clinical, sexy, and disturbing phrase.

"So, I need to pass it straight to you?"

"Basically, yes. To a doctor, who will inject it." She picked at her fingernails. She's all nerves and fidgets. "They say my body rejects anything that isn't fresh. They're not sure why, but they're telling me this is the only way I can conceive."

She looked around, making sure no one overheard our conversation. The cougars were still basking in the far corner of the room, drinking martinis and whispering to one another in the hot tub.

We both played some cards. We both have a few left. I laid my king on the table. "I don't mean to be insensitive. But I'll need more money. It was an incredibly challenging decision last time. And it's getting more personal and much more difficult."

She laid a tender hand on mine, pleased with my response. The first real smile I'd seen since I showed up tonight. "I'm not concerned about money, Vick. I want a child. Does that mean you'll do it?"

"Sure. I'll do it. But I need one-fifty this time. Double-duty, double pay." Am I negotiating right now? I'm so proud of myself I could dance an Irish jig.

"Done. I'll text the legal team and have it sent over right now." She whipped out her phone and started pecking at the screen.

One hundred fifty thousand dollars is a lot of money, maybe even enough to buy another property. With another paid-off property, I'm only a few years away from an early retirement.

She hugged me. She wiped the tears free and laughs, "I'm so excited! Oh, thank you!" and then she hugged me again. Lines of makeup were dry on her cheeks. She looked halfway decent again, back to normal except for the painted Indian face, which, could be hot if you're into that kinda thing. Her phone buzzed. She checked it and says, "It's ready. They'll be here in ten minutes."

"Ten minutes?" I swig my champagne, finishing it. "Were they waiting down the road? It takes at least thirty minutes from the city."

"They aren't driving, Vick." A mischievous smile. "I have a surprise for you."

CHAPTER TWENTY-EIGHT

The rotor blades were loud, much louder than I remember. It'd been a long time since I'd been this close to a landing helicopter. The wind kicked up pebbles and ice. They stung as they pelted my arms and face. Alexa was faced away from the landing chopper, on her phone. She was immune to how impressive it was.

It touched down gently on the snow-covered ground. One of her beer-bellied attorneys hunched below the blades, exiting onto the icy helipad. He held a briefcase, passing it to Alex with a wave. It was far too loud to talk so she used a thumbs-up to say *thanks*, or *good to go*, or whatever.

She crouched, walking below the blades and approached the cabin. She slid on a pair of headphones, sat down, and waved to me. Wait. What? I pointed to myself, then to the helicopter. She nodded. The wind from the engine is furious, louder than a rumbling train. It's been years since I'd been in a bird. Since the military.

I leaned down, sliding beneath the spinning blades and boarded. She passed me a pair of headphones and I slid them on.

"Let's celebrate, Vick!" Her voice sounded mechanical through the headset. Celebrate? I have a sitter at home. I shouldn't be going anywhere. Then again, fuck it. I'll give her double her normal babysitting rate. How can I pass up a ride?

"Where are we going?" I pulled the door closed with a thud I could feel but not hear.

"You'll see." She got the attention of the pilot and pointed up.

It was a feeling I'd forgotten. The woozy, gravity-defying teeter-totter of lifting vertically from Earth. The helicopter was newer than any I'd been in. It had leather cushioned seats and wood-paneled walls in the rear. There was even a flat screen TV in the wall. It certainly wasn't a spacious interior, but it felt luxurious, unlike the scratched steel paneled interior of the war birds I rode in over the desert.

We stayed airborne for a while. She watched me the entire time. Not occasionally, no-no, she watched me through the trip's entirety. I wasn't paying too much attention though. I caught her gaze when I took a break from watching the view. The city was beautiful. A winter wonderland of brightly lit buildings and cul-de-sac Christmas lights. I love this time of year. I'll trade beaches and mai tais for blizzards and sledding any day.

We landed gently at the airport on a freshly plowed runway. Kudos to the pilots for a steady descent and perfect landing. I wonder how much the Livingstons pay for a helicopter on standby?

I don't recognize this side of the airport. We landed at the far end of the runway near a few hangars that appeared unused. From what I've seen, the airlines generally congregate, forming tightly knit anthills of activity. This wasn't that.

Two other helicopters were parked on big letter H's next to the hangars. Blue lights glowed from the cracks in the massive hangar doors. We hopped off and immediately the helicopter lifted and disappeared into the sky. I shrugged, confused, pointing to the departing helicopter. *Where the fuck is he going?*

"C'mon. They'll be back," Alex yelled and grabbed my hand. She'd fixed her makeup just before we landed, so she was back to her normal intimidatingly put-together self.

We entered through a side door on hangar number thirty-four. A black guy sat behind a desk and barely lifted his head as we entered. Alex stopped in front of him, putting her hands on the desk.

"Octopus."

He lifted his head from his book, made eye contact, stuck two fingers in his mouth, and whistled like a fat guy at a Little League game. A white guy in a black hat popped his head around the corner. "Name."

"Alexa and Victor Miller."

The guy checked his list. A thin, battered clipboard held a few flipping pages. "Yes, yes. Welcome, Mr. and Mrs. Miller. These guys will escort you to VIP." He stamped our wrists with a red octopus.

More of them now. Four guys appeared from a side room. All of them in black uniforms, bulletproof vests, and tactical cargo pants. These guys were security, heavy security, from the looks of 'em. They weren't fucking around with pepper spray and polite words either, they carried rifles.

We followed them. Rather, we followed two of them while two followed us. We were surrounded by a blanket of security. Feels nice to be special. One door led to two, then a hallway. I heard music. Some kind of wild beat. Just the bass like that terrible dance music I hear the neighbor kids playing.

Umph, umph.

It got louder as we wound through the next hallway.

Thump, thump.

Stickers from various bands were stuck to all of the walls. The lights were dimmer now. And different colors. Red. Then blue. One of the guards pushed a few stoned, green-haired kids out of the way as we approached.

Bump, bump, bump.

They opened a door at the end of the hall.

Boom! Boom! Boom!

I could feel the loud music in my chest. The last door opened, exposing the entire hangar, decorated in purple lights and strobing LED lights. Hundreds of people danced and jumped in tune with the beat. It stinks of bleach, perfume, and cigarette smoke.

Boom! Boom! Boom!

The crowd is young. Mostly twenties and pockets of thirties. All kinds of people danced. Asian, black, white, red. Purple hair, green and yellow. Painted. Drunk. Stoned or just plain excited, all of them danced and hopped around like they'd never heard music.

Alex stopped the platoon outside at an ice bar, just past a massive totem pole, the kind of thirty-foot pole I saw in Norway. Painted faces and monsters carved into the side, climbing eagerly to the top.

"Purple Passion X!" Alex said to the bartender, loud enough to be heard over the thumping music. She made a peace sign with her hand and yelled, "Two of them!"

Boom! Boom! Boom!

I was yelling, "Alex, I need to go soon… maybe half an hour?" I do. I know I sound old and crotchety but it's getting late. I've got a precious kid who is sleeping and a wife who's passed out. She placed a finger on my lips.

Boom! Boom! Boom!

"Shhhhhhhh, Professor. Give me an hour. Let's have some fun. Celebrate!" She pulled the glowing purple drinks across the bar and slid one to me. She grinned and slid the straw through a slit between her lips.

I watched her drink. Then I watched a slithering, half-naked dancing girl in a cage suspended from the ceiling. "One hour. Fine. But then we need…" Fuck. She did it again. Same finger. Same shush noise. This time followed with a straw. She handed me my drink and shoved the straw in my mouth.

Boom! Boom! Boom!

Tasted pretty good. Like a piña colada and something else. Good. Damn good. I sucked down a bit more. My nerves weren't as fried as they were earlier, thanks to the champagne, but I could feel this purple cookie or whatever the fuck it's called working its magic.

Boom! Boom! Boom!

The guards pushed through the crowd, creating a wide, safe path for us. I felt my neck loosen. My shoulders lost their tightness. She turned, looking back at me, still sipping her purple thingy. I hate this music, but it feels different somehow. I can feel it now. In my chest and in my heart. It feels good. My heart pumps in rhythm with the bass. It's energy — pure energy! Adrenaline! A smile slips across my face. A careless smile I vaguely remember from the days of the past.

Boom! Boom! Boom!

A long red velvet rope was lifted as we approach a secluded part of the hangar. The folks past the ropes aren't dressed like the raving, hippy kids in the crowd. This group is dressed well. Classier. Like the guys at the party we just left. Mostly expensive tuxedos, dresses, and suits. Some danced. Some didn't. Mostly they sat at tables, watching the madness behind crystal glasses of glowing liquid.

Our security squad broke off and stood along the velvet lines. They weren't the only security. Ten or so black hats also stood at the line, protecting it like the Tijuana border.

Boom! Boom! Boom!

I can't remember the last time my head felt this clear or the last time I've felt this alive. It's like I'm seeing color for the first time after years of monochrome. A waiter, also dressed in a tux, sat us at a small red table and brought a bloated bottle of vodka and a tray of pills. She winked and slid one of the tiny white pills onto her tongue. She flicked her tongue at me, showing me the pill just before she swallowed it.

Fuck, she dosed me. I looked at what was left of my glowing purple drink. What secrets do you hold, purple thing? Am I mad? I feel too damn good to be mad. Every nerve ending is blasting with an orgasmic tingle. I haven't felt this calm and carefree in... years.

Boom! Boom!

CH9PTER 2WENTY-N9NE

"I need a picture of our big moment. Do you mind?"

He lifts his phone and snaps an image of me. I need *both* of us, love, both of us. Though I did pose. Maybe he will frame it someday.

"No, of us! Today isn't about me. It's about us, making something magical. Something very special." He walks toward me. He's really doing it. I feel his hand on the side of my hip. His arm wrapped snugly around my waist. Does he feel the sweat? Does he feel the moist glow oozing from my pores? Control your breaths and stop being nervous. Victor Miller is touching me. *Me*. Breathe. He snaps the picture.

"Can you send those to me? You have my direct line."

"As soon as I am done in the clinic, I'll send it over."

"Please!" Vick. I can't take the suspense. What if you forget? What if I never get my hands on this picture? The first time we touched. The first documented photo of us together. "Please send it now." Send it, *send it, send it!*

Yes. *Sigh* — he will. He agrees. I give him my number again. I can't believe my luck when I feel my phone buzz in my purse. I wanted him to take the photos because I want his hand doing the work and I want those images saved in his collection.

"Perfect. Just, perfect! Oh, you look just like him. It's… uncanny. You look amazing."

I thank him again and shake his hand, *his* hand, *Vick's hand!* After I watch him enter the clinic, I skip back to the elevators. I'm just feet from my Victor as he pleasures himself. He is touching his penis right *now*, right *there* for *me!* Oh my God! This is incredible! I look at the picture of us. His arm around my body, smiling into the camera.

I immediately frame the picture. I frame several actually. They are blown-up images of perfection, singing to me from the walls of room 9. Every time I enter I see us together. A strong reminder. A reminder my work is paying off. The plan is working. Drink the water, Vick!

I sent Javier, my very gay and very good, personal shopper, out for lotto tickets as I've done every day for the last few weeks. I've amassed 6,000 dollars' worth of scratch-off tickets. At night, I scratch. I scratch and I throw them into 1 of 3 piles. The larger pile holds the duds. The losers. The Krayas. The peasant tickets, worth less than the paper they're printed upon.

The middle pile is the mini-winners. Tickets that won mere dollars. Maybe 10. Nothing substantial enough to catch my attention. The third pile was for the big winners. The exciting pile. So far I'd hit several 100-dollar wins and a few 500 dollar.

It'd become a nightly routine. Finish at the office, go to the club, work out, hit the spa, eat dinner, have a glass of wine, and scratch off more tickets. Of course, I still keep close tabs on him throughout the day. My phone chirps and vibrates when he is on the move. I'll pet his face on the screen as I watch the scattered surveillance cameras. Isn't he lovely?

I found time to get other things done, too. Tasks I've had on my list for far too long. I added hair removal cream to Kraya's conditioner, careful not to contaminate Vick's nearby bottle. The thought of his precious hair being poisoned — ugh! What a nightmare. I bought Vick a brand new bottle of shampoo, too, to make sure he didn't run out and use hers.

I had another draft of the contract written and an anal bleaching treatment. The girls at the club rave about it. They were right. Things are cleaner and Vick will love it.

I'd been dreading this moment though. I hadn't seen Vick in weeks and it'll be another 13 days until the party. If there is ever a time, it is now. It will heal by then.

Every time I see him, I sweat. My forehead glows. My thighs tingle and my armpits drool. Disgusting, unforgiving, wet, pooling sweat under my arms. The inside of my sleeves are always soaked when I'm finished with him. There is only one solution. One. I've tried expensive deodorant and I've tried lasers and medication.

The spoon is red hot. Vick's face encourages me from the walls of room 9. I watch him on the screens. He's on the couch, watching TV at his house. Kraya is sleeping, as usual. Peasant cunt. She can't bring herself to sit by him? Talk to him? If she only knew how lucky she is. Or was.

The torch, a standard blue flamed tool from the hardware store, has been blowing fire on this spoon for 5 minutes. This is the moment. I hold the vanilla bottle tightly. Clench my teeth against cloth and press the smoldering spoon into my armpit.

I hear the sizzle and I feel the burn of my nerves shrieking and dying against the fiery heat. I grit harder and shriek, watching Vick on the couch. "Never again will I sweat like a pig. You'll see. I'll be perfect for you."

I pull the spoon from my armpit with an open mouth gasp for air. Strings of burnt flesh follow like pizza mozzarella. I whimper muffled yelps behind the shirt in my mouth. I drop the spoon and slap the wet, alcohol-soaked rag onto my burn. Scar tissue cannot open for sweat glands. It closes them off like glue. Alcohol will stop an infection. Lightning and pain strike my armpit and I feel every muscle in my body ignite. The pain is a 10. Maybe a 20 on a scale of 10. My eyes are wide and my skin is bumpy — I've never experienced this much pain. I'm doing this for you, love! One pit done. Now, on to…

The room is getting darker. I can't see his face in the monitor anymore. My thoughts are drowning in the pain, gasping for air. I struggle to stay awake, but I am overcome and the room turns to black…

CHAPTER THIRTY

Boom! Boom! Boom!

What is that noise?

Boom! Boom! Boom!

Is it getting louder?

Boom! Beep. Beep.

My eyes fluttered open and I had a headache so strong I could feel my pulse in my temples.

Beep. Beep.

I sat up in bed. Kraya was beside me, out cold with her legs strangling a pillow. I wiped the crud from my eyes. Yellow pebbles fell onto my chest. What day is it? What time is it?

Beep.

I shuffled to the window. A flatbed tow truck was backing into my driveway, my car asleep on the bed of the truck. Beep, beep, beep. I pulled on some sweatpants and a big jacket, and ran out my front door, nearly tripping over my tired feet.

"Hello! Hi!" I yelled to the tow truck driver. He was out of the cab, unchaining my car. I could see my breath in the winter air. Snow was powdered sugar on my sidewalk.

"Drop off for Victor?" He's greasy. Not just because he is covered in oil — the kind of grease that lingers in the way he dresses and smiles. I nodded. "Sign here, chief." He handed me a yellow piece of paper. I noticed the stamp on my wrist as I grabbed the sheet.

Holy shit. No wonder my head was playing the boom sticks. Is this a new watch on my wrist, too? I signed his paperwork. He walked to the assembly of levers and lowered the car. The hydraulics were loud and shook the car as it tipped to the concrete. Nothing on this machine was quiet.

Bits and pieces, small fragments of the night were coming back to me. I squinted in the morning sun. The cold air hurt my lungs. I remember…

She yelled over the thumping music. Said something like, "I told you I have a surprise for you," and beckoned one of the waiters.

I remember the man, another waiter, I think, bringing a box to our table. It had a fat red ribbon around the outside and a pretty bow. Alex handed it to me, thanking me for helping her again on her quest for fertility.

Inside was a watch. A watch with a teeny crown at the top of the face. A Rolex? Holy shit. I looked at my wrist in the morning light, pulling back the jacket far enough to see the glimmering face. Yep. Rolex.

"All done, Victor." The tow truck driver pulled the last chain from my bumper. "Have a purdy mornin'."

She must have towed my car from Nick's house here. Fuckin' rich people. I've done the walk of shame back to my car at the bar countless times. Never have I thought about sending a tow truck to bring it back for me. Gotta love the way they think.

To my surprise, the doors were unlocked. I opened the passenger side and spot a stack of pages on the seat. A familiar stack, held together with that same struggling paperclip. Looking through the pages, I saw it was signed and dated — all from last night. I rubbed my skull with a furrowed brow. My headache still doing the macarena between my ears.

I started reading. I only lasted a few seconds before I realized it was too damn cold and I needed coffee. I also needed something strong enough to kill the little drummer boy in my head. Probably Ibuprofen.

Kraya was *still* sleeping. The kid, too. The whole house was nestled snugly in their beds. Our Christmas tree smelled amazing, the fresh pine smell that peaks its head around the holiday season. I plugged in the Christmas lights, brewed some coffee, turned on some holiday tunes, and read.

It took a while, but I managed to understand the basics. I needed to go back to the tower soon. I was to "arrive at The Twelfth Floor Clinic at ten-forty a.m., CST on December twenty-ninth..." No rest for the wicked...

I checked my watch, surprised again by the foreign piece of shiny steel. I was expecting my old digital watch with the date at the top in blinking square numbers. I don't know where anything is on this thing.

Francis wore a watch like this. I remember her telling me that. I flash back again, a momentary jogging of memory.

She's sitting across from me, lights still flashing and weirdos still dancing. I was smiling because my body felt about twenty pounds lighter. She asked me if I was enjoying myself. I was. She told me about her late husband. How she adored him. How a child will put everything right in the world. She asked about my wife. If she appreciated me. If she loved me the way I needed her to love me. I remember thinking that was strange, but people tend to get awfully personal after a few purple things.

I grabbed a cup of fresh coffee. I brewed it strong today because I need it. I threw back a few maroon Ibuprofen tablets and sipped coffee from an old mug. Shit — how did I get home? Everything is a blur. Though, not a disgusting blur like a night of too many whiskey shots. A thrilling blur with twists and turns and helicopter rides and dancing women in cages.

Holy shit. Alexa was dancing, too, next to our table. A seductive, twisting choreograph of legs and skin. It flashes, bits of memory coming together in a strobe of images. She didn't dance with me though. With someone else. Who was that someone else? Think. What happened?

It was a woman. Yes! A younger woman with a nice yellow sundress and black hair. They held hands, grinding torso to butt. Skin everywhere. Do I remember them kissing? Damn! I can't remember it clearly. Maybe it's safer if I forget.

I spot a pool of hair on the floor. Kraya's hair. I remember that now, too. I hear cries from the baby's room. He's waking up.

CHAPTER THIRTY-ONE

Christmas morning came and went. The kiddo ran downstairs, stuffed puppy (Pup-pup) in hand, excited to see the tree and the enchantments beneath. Kraya was too tired to come downstairs. I made pancakes, bacon, and eggs and the two of us had breakfast. I had to chop it up for the lad, of course.

I waited two hours before Kraya graced us with her presence. She drifted in and out of consciousness on the couch as Junior and I opened the green and red gift boxes. Wrapping paper flew wildly around the room as he opened his new toys. After lunch, Kraya livened up enough to give me a gift.

A tall, foiled box with a card that read, *Merry Christmas, Vick. I love you.* I ripped open the paper and peered inside at a glimmering new lamp. A lamp — yes — a lamp. Things haven't been the same since Kray took a turn. She has good days and bad. Mostly no bueno.

On the really bad days, I drink. I'll start with an early morning cocktail and leave the pub at five. I usually limit myself to four or five drinks. She's not just sick, she's turned into a black hole of negativity and sleepiness. I drink to relax. I drink to forget the problem at home that lives in my wife. My beautiful, wonderful wife who's shifted toward something icky. It's temporary, I remind myself, and she'll be back to normal. The docs promise me this.

The doctors still say it's post-pregnancy anxiety and depression. Can last up to four years, they say. Awesome. Sign me up! After the worst Christmas I can remember, I tried to set her up with yet another appointment. *This cannot be normal. There must be a solution; more medication? Or maybe less medication? Something.* Anything that can bring my wife back from the zombie that's inhabited her body.

Of course, the doctor's office is crazy this time of year. Christmas break and New Years are unforgiving.

I check my watch — December twenty-ninth. I switched back to the digital watch. It's easier to read and a lot lighter. I sold the Rolex on eBay for a fortune. A fortune I turned around and invested into bills and paying down properties.

Today is the day I drop back into the tower for one of two more deposits. I hate to admit I'm excited. I have a hop in my step. Not for the fun part (although the tug on a rug won't be terrible), but for the paycheck. Things have been pretty tight since Kraya has been understandably unhelpful. I've had to hire an in-home babysitter, not a cheap one either.

I excused myself, passing the torch of responsibility to the babysitter, and left the house. My car was still warm from the earlier trip to the grocery store. I pulled out of the garage and almost clipped the passenger mirror on the doorframe.

I whistled a Christmas tune while I drove. My new tires gripped the road well, despite the fresh ice. I parked near the front door at the tower, next to a row of handicapped spots.

I checked in at the front desk, that same marble monstrosity I'd visited a few times prior. The girl I talked to last time wasn't there. A fresh crop of headset-wearing ladies waited for me to approach. Before I could speak, the brunette on the left called to me: "Mr. Victor Miller?"

"Yes." Am I becoming a regular at Livingston Tower? Pretty cool.

"Mr. Miller, please follow Mr. Needle. He will escort you to your appointment." She pointed to my favorite little man.

"Mr. Miller. Come with me please." He was as delightful this time as he was the last. We looped through the familiar halls to the elevator. He pressed the number twelve with a feeble finger, smiling smugly in place of casual conversation. I tried to converse, I really did, but he didn't respond. The classic "Let it Snow," by Bing Crosby, played over the speaker in the elevator.

The door chimed. When it opened, Mr. Needle pointed to The Twelfth Floor Clinic. I exited and he (again) didn't. His expression didn't change as he lifelessly pushed the elevator button. He kinda reminded me of a toy robot with a low battery. What a charmer.

I introduced myself at the counter. This time I did recognize some people. A few of the same receptionists were here. I recognize the doc, too. "Did you miss me?" I extend a hand.

"Sure," he said, shaking my hand with a dead-fish grip. "Welcome back, Mr. Miller." We entered a different door this time. He unlocked it by pressing his ID card to a panel. "Do you understand the procedure we are going to do today, Mr. Miller?"

I walked past several rooms with different colored lights above the doors. "I mast..." I looked around to make sure none of the nurses or patients who lingered in the hallway could hear me. I whispered, "I masturbate in a cup, hand it to you, and you give it to Alex?"

He looked back at me, stethoscope bouncing every other step. "Miss Livingston, yes. You are aware we are all going to be in close proximity? Privacy will be at a minimum, Mr. Miller."

CHAPTER THIRTY-TWO

He opened the last door in the final stretch of the hallway. One big room housing two beds, a doctor, a suited fat guy I'd never met, and Alex. "Mr. Miller is here, Dr. Mackelby." Was that necessary? It was pretty obvious I was there now. The room was unexpectedly small, a smidge larger than my bedroom. It's decorated with a desk, two beds, a multicolored plastic skeleton, and a scale. The two beds separated only by a hospital curtain.

That's it? A *shower curtain*? I've gotta perform in *this* room?

"Thanks for coming, Vick." She was lying on the opposing bed. The suit handed me a few forms to sign. I read through the first few lines. He pointed to the plastic "sign here" tabs. My pen scratched my signature on the page. My pen is the only sound in the small room and I felt like everyone was looking at me. They were.

I signed next to the last red arrow and handed the metallic clipboard back to him. I didn't read it. It looked standard and I panicked with all the eyeballs on my back. I saw a confidentiality agreement, a hold harmless, blah, blah... The doc who brought me into the room told me to sit on the bed behind the curtain. I could still see Alex and the others across the room, no farther than a stone's throw.

He handed me a small plastic cup, a magazine, and asked me if I was ready.

"You guys get right down to business, don'tcha!" Holy hell I feel rushed.

"We only have a small ovulation and temperature window, Mr. Miller." The doc started closing the curtain. He asked, "Is there anything else?"

"I'm good. Thanks, Doc."

"Please begin," he said as he closed the curtain. Small talk couldn't have hurt anything, consider it foreplay. I hadn't caught up with Alex since the party. I suppose this is the result she wanted, no need to schmooze me anymore.

I pulled myself out and began doing what I do. It was difficult to concentrate with all that silence on the other side. They were all listening. I tried my best to keep it silent, but I wasn't getting hard. Someone cleared their throat.

I've never milked the moose with an audience. *C'mon. C'mon. No pressure. Just act like nobody's there. No biggy.* I heard the door on the other side. It opened and closed.

"Do you need better visual stimulation, Mr. Miller?" I heard from across the line. I could see their feet under the curtain.

"No. I'm fine." *Fuckers — shut up! C'mon. C'mon.* I tried to clear my head. Closed my eyes. Tried to think of nothing, just focused on the way it felt — the warmth of my hand sliding around and the way a release would feel. I made it to half-mast, just a few seconds from a full salute. It was all downhill from there, baby.

"Is there anything we can do for you, Mr. Miller? To make it go faster?" the doc said.

"Yes. You can shut up! Pretend I'm not here, Doc. Stop talking!" For Christ's sake, Doc. Seriously?

I needed to start over again. I started polishing and did my best to tune out the world. I closed my eyes, cup in my left hand, and rocket in my right. Wax on. Wax off. Easy.

Some ass-hamper clears his throat again. *C'mon. C'mon.* I keep at it. A minute passed. I was close, almost to the boiling point. *Ignore them and focus on how it feels —* they're a million miles away.

I was too close to care anymore. I was about to strike white oil and it didn't bother me if they heard it. I'm a pair of mumbling, flailing pigeon toes below the curtain. I stopped, looked at the cup, and I was pretty proud of myself.

Both docs barged in unexpectedly. I stowed my baggage and handed them the cup. One of them used a rubber turkey baster thingy to suck up the spaff. The other held the cup like it was a ticking bomb, keeping it level and safe. God forbid he drops it and I have to make another hundred G's.

They whipped open the rest of the curtain and rushed to Alex's side. Then, I heard it. Words I never expected to hear today.

"Vick. Come here…"

She called me to her side again. It's surreal; a moment so strange, exotic, and natural, I could never have predicted how I'd react. I walked toward her.

"It's beautiful."

She lay on the bed, legs spread with a thin blue sheet over her chest and thighs. Her open hand stretched far off the bed, inviting me to be a part of her miracle.

I was standing next to her then, and not sure how I got there. I should leave. This has gotten far too personal! Too intimate. She gently wrapped her hand around mine and whispered, "Incredible, isn't it?"

The doctors moved back the sheet, making room to work with the turkey baster syringe. The blanket glided up her knees, past her thighs and stopped just below her bellybutton. I politely turned away.

"It's okay, Vick." She released her grip from my hand and pulled my chin to watch. "It's life. It's beautiful! There is nothing to be ashamed of here."

Okay. Okay. I am a mature adult. She is right. There is nothing to be ashamed of. I tried to be mature, tried to watch the beauty without distraction. But I'm distracted. My attention followed her hairless, tan thighs into a triangular patch of pleasure below her manicured pubic region. I watch as they slowly slid it inside her. Deeper. I felt her hand around my arm again. She was squeezing this time, whispering something. I couldn't hear her; I was too fixated on the gliding penetration.

She whispered again, hand growing tighter on my elbow. The doctor squeezed the plunger and the semen pushed from the clear plastic tube inside her. I felt her nails in my skin and I heard her then. I heard her whispering so quietly, so intensely, only I could hear it. I turned and saw her eyes focused intensely on me.

"I'm cumming, Vick..."

CHAPTER THIRTY-THREE

I've experienced joys and deaths in my life and I've encountered surprises on too many continents. Those words though, along with the nails in my arm, stunned me. Like, loss of minor motor skills stunned. Her legs trembled and her eyes rolled back in her head. The docs didn't notice, or at least didn't act like they noticed.

We talked briefly after the incident. Mostly we discussed the party, my payment, and the contract. We talked about everything *except* the part about the unexpected orgasm. It was a casual exchanging of pleasantries and goodbyes. She was back to her old self. Cold, hot, Alexa.

It was all I could think about. I went home, showered, and donated again — this time to the bathtub drain. That body. Light bronze, quivering thighs, and a patch of perfectly trimmed pelvic hair. Her whisper and her claws. I'm a teenager again, fixated on a woman with an intensity only puberty could understand.

Kraya sat with us at dinner. Both of us chewed our food in a daze. The little dude ate playfully, blissfully unaware of the rights and wrongs beneath our roof. I thought about my vows — "Till death do us part. In sickness and in health." Even sick and blank, she is still my wife. I have needs though. I wonder if she does, too. Does she think about sex anymore?

The following day came quickly. And so did I. Same room, same docs. Same Alexa, hiding behind the curtain. The events played out the same, but when the time came, I did not stand at her side. She called to me again, but I stood idle near the doorway when the plastic syringe pushed inside her body. She didn't climax this time. Her feet didn't twist in the leg rests. She accepted my seed without emotion. She watched me as they emptied the tube.

I'd requested cash instead of other methods of payment. I wanted this to stay off the radar in case Kraya suddenly became aware enough to review our finances. Someone inside me wanted her back, back to our normal world of stupid jokes and cuddly late-night movies. The little guy outside of me didn't. He was hard for Alex.

I took the envelope. One hundred fifty thousand in cash isn't as heavy as I thought it would be. It felt insignificant. Cash will also help me avoid those pesky questions from the IRS when they came clawing for their cut of my dirty work. Were they there to encourage me when the docs weren't? No. It was just willy and me... and Alex.

CHAPT3R THIRTY-4OUR

"Last time you were here..." She opens her notebook and skimmed a few lines. "You told me your husband has been acting strange. You also mentioned he has been seeing someone else?" She is a professional at open-ended questions. I feel my fingers picking at each other. Stop fidgeting and breathe. You can handle this.

"Yes. He has." Good. Good answer. See, you're doing a great job, no need to be intimidated by the ugly girl at the dance.

She writes more. Her pen scratches ink onto the page in the quiet office. It's hard not to notice the bland wallpaper and her distressed oak desk. On the desk, a variety of red, blue, and black pens sat neatly in a "World's Greatest Mom" mug. Does she have vodka in her bottom drawer? Does she tire of listening to problems all day, day in and day out?

Her pen scrapes the page. "Do you know the woman?" she asks.

"I know her, yes."

"Does it upset you that he is having an affair?"

"He isn't cheating!" I feel my heartbeat behind my eyes again. I wipe the first drop of sweat from my forehead.

Moisture builds on my brow. "He is just..." In my lap, my pointer finger quickly traces circles on a fingernail. "I don't know, experimenting!" I pause and adjusted my skirt again. "Once he finds out how much I love him, he'll love me."

"Do you think it's a healthy relationship if he is seeing other people?" she said and lifted her eyes from the notepad, ready to analyze my response.

"No! Of course it's not healthy, but we've always had an interesting relationship. This is just... just... just another curveball." Stop! Stop feeding her. Short answers, remember? Short — controlled — answers.

She jots more notes. "Does he know you know about her?"

"Does he know? *Does he know*?"

I wipe my brow. My makeup runs, tears welling, mutilating my mascara. Control yourself. Don't let go. Don't lose control again. I forgot how hard it is to come here.

The therapist slides a box of tissues across the table. "Tell me about that."

Pins and needles in my mouth. I purse my lips so tightly they are numb. I snatch a tissue from the box and wipe black smudges from my cheeks. How did this happen to *me*? To *us*? I hate him for it, but I can't live without him. His touch and his laugh and his... everything!

"We'll save that for later..." She scribbles more on the page. "Does he know you're struggling? Taking medication?"

Words are trapped. My mouth opens but my throat is too tight to make a sound. My palms are wet. "No," I squeak.

"Last time you were here, you told me you felt invisible. Like his life is being lived without you. Do you still feel this way?"

My throat is hard around the spit I tried to swallow, like a snake squeezing my neck from the inside. Why are you pushing me, bitch? — "Yes..." My eyes meet hers. Rage — sadness — Oh my God, I'm too vulnerable.

More scribbling. "Does he know about your condition? Your history? Your..." She leans forward. "...your mental health history?"

I see you.

I see you watching me from behind your coffee table. I feel your judgment. I know you. You're like all the others. *I seeeeeeeeeeee you.* No! Not today. "No, he doesn't know about my history." I'm so vulnerable. Why did I come back here? Check, please. Check, please! I'm done. Done! I should have never talked to anyone about this. Who do you think you are? You're a peasant therapist with certificates from a *state school* and a 2-dollar barn painting on the wall. I stand and walk to her side of the table. She leans back with a smug, uncomfortable smile. "And no one else should know about my condition."

The knife feels sticky as it slides into her neck. Her eyes watch mine: predator and prey. She got too close — Why did you have to do that? Look what you've done! Why didn't you let me talk about him, or let me talk about my day and about how much I love him? Or you could have asked me *why* I love him. Or, or, or, or tell me he will run to me and he will love me! He doesn't want that other woman. *I am the only one for him.* You did this to yourself, Counselor. You should have played nice.

She tries to yell but it is just bubbles and gurgling. "You don't know about my condition..." I pull the blade from her skin. — "...anymore."

She slumps back in her chair, holding her neck with a goofy, surprised expression. You should have known I'd bark back, bitch. Her eyes turn off, leaving her with a final, dim, expressionless gaze. She looks pretty now.

No stress. No judgment. It suits her well.

Oh my gosh. *Oh my gosh.* Vick. What have I done? *Stop fidgeting!* I did this for you. For us. She deserved it, sneaky bitch. Look what happens when you dip your toe in the deep end, Counselor. What have I done?

Focus. Think. This is no time to panic. Now is not the time. I grab her computer and her calendar from the top of her desk. I snag her bottle of hand sanitizer, too, knocking her mommy mug to the floor with a crash. With both arms full, I leave through the side door.

Good — perfect! He is still there. A homeless man in his sixties (or maybe his thirties with a lot of narcotics) is still sleeping under the concrete bench. My car is a few paces from him, facing east in the lot. I put the laptop on the roof of my car and fumble through my purse. I always lose these things, dammit. Where are my keys? I find the black key fob and push the trunk button. I drop the therapist's schedule and laptop into the trunk. I unzip my first-aid kit and put on purple medical gloves. Not because I am too worried about DNA (although that is a cute ancillary benefit), but because I have to touch him. This, this… vagrant. A disease that grows on my streets. I am careful not to wake the bum under the bench while I wipe the bloody knife on his sleeve.

I make sure to get some on his right hand, especially under his fingernails. He smells putrid, like alcohol and infection. I tuck her purse into his filthy camouflage jacket and wrap the strap around his neck.

I go back to my car and reach into the glove box. Insurance cards, some napkins and 3 tampons fall to the floor mat. Is it still in here? Of course it is. The phone is on a battery charger, stuck with Velcro to the back of the glove compartment. It's the burner phone I use to call Vick and hang up. I've called him many times, to hear him say hello. I purchased it with cash at a convenience store a few blocks from the tower. I power it on and dial the short number.

"Nine-one-one, what is your emergency?" The dispatcher's voice is professional and monotone.

"Oh my gosh, I... I... I saw a man! A man screaming and yelling and covered in blood! Covered! He looks like a crazy person, a... a... a maniac!" I said.

"Ma'am, calm down. Can you tell me where you are?" the police dispatcher asked.

"I... I... I don't know! I think on 9th Avenue near that big brown apartment building?" I know damn well where I am. I built that apartment complex last year and I know none of the cameras work on the south side — on *this* side. Why didn't we repair them? Why should we — ghettos stay ghetto.

Why should I keep throwing money at a building that keeps trying to knock itself down?

"Ma'am, you're doing fine. Officers are on their way now. What does the man look like?"

Shit. I need to move. "He is in a... a... an army jacket. He looks crazy! Ahhhhh! He is covered in blood! Ahhhhh! He is *coming this way!*" I hang up and pop the battery out from the back of the phone case. Now the fun part. I pull the two epinephrine pens from under my arm and walk back to the bum. His scab-ridden calf is exposed, sunburnt and covered in cuts. I slam the needles into the meaty part of his leg, injecting enough adrenaline into his system to send him to the moon. His eyes flutter open. I snag the needles and put the cap back on, careful not to stick myself with his disease. He screams and panics. I stuck him with enough adrenaline to pick up a car. I ditch the pens and the burner phone battery in the rusty gutter and run back to my car. I fumble with my keys again. I hear sirens — they're getting closer. I pull my seatbelt across my chest, start the car, and drive away casually as the flashing lights approach. Police officers pulled guns on the man in my rearview mirror. He is running in circles, trying to burn off the adrenaline cocktail.

Pop! Pop-pop-pop!

The transient man is a slumped mess of red in the mirror. Did they shoot him? Was that a car backfiring? Shit, shit, *shit!*

My hands are shaking on the wheel. Fuck, that was close. Why did I do that? Why? I need to keep control. *Focus.* No more distractions. I thought I was done with incidents like this. Those days are far behind me. I splash a few pumps of hand sanitizer on my shaky palms, wiping the blood smears with tissue. I need to be more careful.

CHAPTER THIRTY-FIVE

Nick Preston sat across from me at the Orchard Club. We smoked cigars and watched the snow fall on the fairway. This was our second meeting. The first time we met, it was all personal, no professional stuff. He asked about my family, my investments. What I thought about the presidency and what book I'd read last. He was testing the water, making sure I wasn't some schlep looking to score, which was exactly what I was, but he seemed to enjoy my company. He threw me a bone and watched what I did when I chewed it. He must have approved because here we were again. A large, stone fireplace fed us warmth as we drank scotch from the leather seats.

"You believe the rental market is still climbing?" Nick took a sip of whiskey and knocked the ash from his cigar.

"I do. I've been pulling numbers from the B&Bs, hotels, and apartment rentals. I have a few guys that send me their sales data. It's climbing all right."

I've been doing my homework. Kraya's been a ghost for as long as I can remember, staying in our room, mumbling and sleeping. I've been occupying my time with work. I do a lot of kiddo stuff, then work in a nap here and there, and then more business. I found guys from all over town to send me their monthly sales data. I threw them a hundred bucks. Poor bastards were stuck making minimum wage at some hotel. A hundred bucks was a big deal to them.

Nick's fingers rested on his chin. His mind busy as he gazed into the popping fire. "I'd like to try something else with you, Victor." He didn't lose eye contact with the burning logs. "I'd like to propose something. A joint venture." Eyes finally joining mine. "I'd like to create a company together. An LLC. I'll fund three million into the company if you can assure the gains. Big gains. Call it twenty percent in the first calendar year?"

That scotch must be strong. "Twenty percent is too aggressive, Mr. Preston." It was. I think he was testing me again — checking to see if I was made of big promises and small returns.

"A most valid concern. My eyes can be larger than my stomach sometimes." He shifted in his seat, paused, and puffed on the stogie. "How about five percent promised returns, and everything above that, you keep?"

Rich guys like Preston don't need to make more money. It's the chase, the control, and the action they need. Five percent is just a point or two higher than the interest he'd get with a big, private firm if he were to park the money somewhere safe. He just wants to play.

"I can live with five percent if we add a guaranteed stipend of seventy thousand for an operations manager."

"I can live with that." He stretched a wrinkled palm toward me. I shook it. "I'll have the lawyers draft something and send it over. I'd like to start no sooner than twelve weeks."

"Twelve weeks is good. I have a few others things I need to finish first." I don't have squat for twelve weeks, but I didn't want to sound desperate. Desperation is about as subtle as a shart.

We sat for a while after the handshake and gazed into the wide fireplace. He stayed put until his wife called him about a concert she wanted to attend. I can't imagine the headache with dating someone half my age. Worried about lip gloss and strawberry daiquiris instead of mortgage payments and hemorrhoid cream. Ah, to be young again.

I smothered my cigar in the big round ashtray and slurped the rest of my drink. I didn't much care for scotch, but if I am going to walk like a duck, I need learn how to quack like one and drink like one, too.

I stuck around for about twenty minutes after he left. I grabbed my jacket, tipped the bartender, and picked up my car from the club valet. These guys know how to live, don't they?

I pulled up to my house in time to catch the babysitter emptying the trash. She waved. I waved. I parked in the driveway instead of the garage and headed to the front door. Snow crunched beneath my shoes and wind burned my cheeks. The trash can needed to be moved to the street, Vanessa. But I don't pay you to clean or push this thing to the avenue, I pay you to make sure my kid doesn't die when I'm gone for the day, so I forgive you. My hands burned on the trash can handle as I rolled it down the drive. I'd fallen down on the ice a few weeks ago while taking out the trash so I take small, flat, shuffle steps. This thing is heavier than usual. What the heck did we do this week? And how do we always have so much trash? Bags were flowing past the lid like the foam on an over-poured lager. Foil caught my eye.

I opened the lid, pulling a cold white grocery bag from near the top. The bag wasn't tied tightly and it was puking cardboard cards, scratch off lottery tickets, packed so tightly the bag was nearly solid. I ripped the bag open, grabbed a fistful, and pulled them out. Scratched, all of them. Hundreds of them, maybe thousands. Three or four drop to my feet. *What. The. Actual. Fuck?*

I slammed a handful of scratchers back into the trash. I leaned down and snatched a few more from the ground. Winners, two of them are ten-dollar winners. Kraya, in her blasted state is gambling our money away and to make matters worse, she is too fucked up to know which ones are winners and which aren't! This is where our money has been going? All of those withdrawals?

I snatched the bag and got back in my car. The first ticket I check is a dud. Second, no bueno. Third, not a winner, and so on until the twelfth ticket. Winner, fifteen dollars. I set it aside. I did this for an hour and forty minutes in the cab of my car. So many tickets in my car it looks like confetti. Overall, I find two thousand eight hundred ten dollars in winning tickets amongst the losing pile.

Are there more bags in the trash? What about last week's pickup?

CHAPT36 THIRTY-6IX

"Good morning, Vick."

"Alex, good morning. What can I do for you?" Vick says.

I see him on the cameras getting up and leaving Kraya at the table. He is sneaking away for me. He is keeping our secret safe. "We should talk."

"We're talking now, aren't we?" I hear myself laugh. I can't believe I let that slip out! Remain professional at all costs. "We are, yes. But we need to discuss some business. Privately."

Stop fidgeting.

I put him on speakerphone. I can feel the depth of his voice in high definition, belting through six or seven speakers throughout the room. He's sitting here with me in room 9 talking to *me*.

He is talking again, the deep vibrations in his voice rumble. He's telling me that he is free next week. No, Vick. You need to stay the course. Stick with *my* plan.

Lips part as I slide his vanilla bottle inside my body. Slow your breathing and control yourself. I tell him the party is tomorrow at 6 p.m. sharp. He needs to pick me up at 5:30 in something formal, something special, something... sharp! He is talking again. I immediately imagine him dressed to the nines, smiling with those perfectly imperfect teeth. His stubble, just long enough to burn as it runs across my skin. My fingers trace my clit. I can see him on the phone in my camera screens.

My back arches on the rubber bed sheets. I switch the camera angle and watch him talking into the phone. On a different monitor I see his wife, eating dinner in the opposing room, eyes glossed, oblivious, drugged out of her gourd. Good girl, Kraya. Stay stupid, peasant. He is still rumbling into the phone. Saying something. I can't focus with these waves of pleasure. *Focus.* Stop fidgeting! You need to respond to him.

I feel myself clench around the vanilla bottle, its rough edges catching the edge of the tender pillows inside me. It's wet. Pulsating. *He is still talking. We're still on the phone and still connected!* I can't wait to see you. I can't wait to hold you. Your body, your smile. Your breath on my chest. I mute the line.

Eruptions are climbing my nerves. I mumble something, enough to answer him. He agrees to pick me up. His words are a deep, rumbling cadence over all the speakers now. I rub harder and trace rhythmic, throbbing circles on my lady lips. *He's coming to pick me up for the party. He's coming!* A guttural yelp escapes my lungs. My hands are shaking, clawing at the sheets. I stare at him on the screen with wide eyes — eyes that haven't blinked. I hear a yell, a pleasured, awkward scream in room 9. A mess of wet and cum and blood and slippery pleasure drips onto the bed. I collapse, writhing in tempo with the slowing electricity in my core.

Click. Vick hangs up.

CHAPTER THIRTY-SEVEN

I bought eight houses with the company Nick and I created. We named it PMI, short for Preston Miller Incorporated. We thought it was clever. I'd previously insisted on Sherlock Homes, LLC, but he wasn't a fan.

I hired a young Asian buck to manage the properties. I paid him forty-five thousand per year and paid myself the other twenty-five thousand to manage him. It was a decent business and it helped that Nick had deep pockets. This was just a hobby for him, a fun ruse to see if we could turn a profit. Must be rough.

I bought smart. The houses had already appreciated in value after a few repairs. I installed new carpet and slapped on a few coats of paint, new doorknobs, and I installed crisp white crown molding. In equity alone we'd made about seventy grand in the first few weeks. Nick was happy. He approached me with another million, but I was losing too much sleep already.

Kraya and I were doing well, especially since I never see her. She spends a lot of time at her therapist's office. They're filling her with antidepressants and gibberish. A lot of good either of those was doing. We barely speak. Rather, she barely speaks. Lifeless eyes and unkempt hair are her only friends now.

Vanessa, our awesome babysitter, was doing a fine job with Junior. I was amazed at how close the two had become. Kraya could barely look at him. She was more concerned with her afternoon naps than feeding him lunch or watching him color. I've considered divorce, of course I have, but I'd feel too guilty to go through with it. She may need me more right now than ever, and I need to continue to be here for her, even if that means to keep the tan line behind my ring.

This time it happened on a Tuesday, when I least expected it. I was in the throne room at one of the properties going number two, reading the back of a paint can with my pants around my ankles. I was startled by the vibration. I leaned down, digging into loose, paint-splattered jeans to find my phone.

The name on the screen meant a lot of things. Probably another payday. Likely another secret from Kraya, and another shot at seeing Alex with her clothes off. I'm comfortable with a few of those. I answered.

"Hi, Vick. Am I catching you at a bad time?"

"It's fine, what can I do for you, Alex?" Well, I have my pants around my ankles because I'm taking a poo, I'm covered in paint, and I have "Every Breath You Take" by The Police blasting on the stereo in an adjacent room. So, nah — not a bad time.

"It's funny, Professor. Isn't it? The routine we've found ourselves in?"

She'd cut through the pleasantries. Unusual, even for Alex. "Yeah…" I'm too curious to hear the rest of the conversation to even try to interpret the oddities that surround this crazy relationship. "Sure it is. It's a good routine, Alex. Helps us both."

"Do you need another specimen?" She must, right? Why else would she be calling me? She doesn't check in, call to chat about the melting snow, or ask about my new businesses. No, she only calls when she needs something. That's our arrangement.

She sighed. A desperate sigh you hear only in defeat. It was obvious she wasn't getting anywhere with the pregnancy. It must be frustrating, especially with the investment she's put into this thing. "Yes. I do." A brief pause on the line. "Do you have a bad connection, Vick? I hear an echo?"

"We must. I'll call you right back." The bathroom was an echo chamber. Classy, dude. Real classy. Why didn't ya just flush, too, while you're at it? Let her hear the whole shebang.

I hiked up my pants and tightened my belt. I barely pooped. At almost forty, it's like Groundhog Day — I never know if he'll retreat or come out for a swim. I turned down the music, pulled out a pad and a pen, then called her back. First ring, she answered.

"Vick?"

"It's not Ghostbusters."

Not a laugh. Not a chuckle. Nothing.

"Vick. We need to talk. Are you free tonight?"

Tonight? It sounded important. Maybe I can have the sitter stay late? I'm going to assume there is money coming my way, so I can foot the bill for more hours, right? Though I do have a hot date with my laptop at seven, then maybe a movie at eight. Cocktails alone in my living room at ten. The usual.

"I'm free tonight, Alex."

"Good. Meet me at Rosenflats at six. Does that work for you, Professor?"

There she goes with that professor garbage again. "The steakhouse? And six-thirty? I'd like to help put the kiddo down for the night." What I lack in understanding and patience, I make up for in good parenting — that's what I tell myself anyway. Being a workaholic doesn't always lend itself well to being a good parent. It's these little white lies we tell ourselves to make the world keep turning.

"Yes, the steakhouse on seventh. Six-thirty is fine. See you there."

"Sounds good. Can you tell me anything about this so I'm not wondering all afternoon?"

"Nope. You'll have to wait to be excited to see me."

Am I? Am I excited to see her? Or is it that I am excited to learn more about a proposal? She wants something, and every time she wants something I get to buy another house. She is making my life easier with every meeting. All for some handsome DNA. "I am excited to see you and learn more." I can say that, right? She won't get the wrong idea? The last thing I need is for her to start thinking I like her and it ruins this business arrangement.

"Great. Thanks, Vick. I'm looking forward to it, too."

The rest of the day flew by. I finished painting and moved my blue tarps to the next room. I looked at myself in the bathroom mirror and spent extra time getting the paint from under my fingernails. What is her offer? What's next? I'm guessing it is another close encounter with the muff kind.

Maybe two rooms, one cup again? Another payday would be timed well — I'm stretched thin this month. My "oh shit fund" is low and the college fund could use a few extra digits. Every extra penny has been invested (or gambled?) into these properties.

I pulled down a few strips of blue painting tape from the freshly colored wall before I left. Blue tape is the worst if you leave it overnight. The house was looking nice, much better than a few weeks ago. I turned off the tunes and the floodlights, grabbed my keys from a bowl I kept on the vacant counter, and pushed the garage door clicker. The garage door is loud and crackles as it winds up. It opened a few feet before it crapped out and stalled. Awesome — just awesome.

CHAPTER THIRTY-EIGHT

The steakhouse is dark. One of those exclusive, snooty, delicious places you visit when you propose to someone or celebrate a new job. Dimmed, hanging lights and dark wood tables are littered throughout. It's bustling with couples sharing wine and coworkers having dinner after work. Most of the waitstaff wore suits while the hostess and waitresses wore almost nothing. I could tell it was expensive from the names of the steaks on the menu out front. When your food is named after something French, or contains more than four words, it's going to cost you.

Seated in a small, private room on the far end of the restaurant was Alex. Well, not just Alex. The Tweedle brothers from our first meeting were also in attendance. Why does she have attorneys with her? Is this good? Just procedure?

Alex hushed when I rounded the corner. Everyone stood and extended polite hands. I shook them all and took a seat. Fine leather met my rump.

"Nice to see you, Alex…" It was nice because she looked nice. Does this broad ever *not* look nice? "You too, fellas." They nodded and we all sat down.

"Thanks for coming, Victor." The black one addressed me first.

Followed promptly by the white one: "We do appreciate you coming on such short notice."

Both of the big boys had those lawyerly, all-knowing, polite smiles you get from someone who knows a secret, but can't tell you. I bet they are about to tell me.

"Good to see you, Vick," Alex said.

"This is infinitely better than a boardroom," I said. I wondered if we were going to eat, or just talk over drinks. Either way, I needed a drink now more than ever. I tried to flag down a passing waitress, but she pretended not to see my raised hand.

"It's been some time since we've seen you, Victor. We've heard great things about your business ventures. How are things for you?" the black one said in an attempt to make casual talk. This guy wants to eat first before diving into business, guaranteed.

"Good. Things are good. Alex here has been throwing me a lot of opportunities." She smiled and sipped her wine. Red, of course.

"You're a natural, Vick. I'm only making a few introductions. Everything else is skill." She is back to flattery. Yep. She wants something.

The waiter, a mid-thirties hipster with a beard and a handlebar mustache approached the table. "How is everyone doing today?" He didn't wait for an answer. "Can I start you off with a drink, Miss? Are we ready to order?"

Finally! Yes! Oh hell yes! Everyone else already has their drinks. The salt and pepper brothers over there are drinking water, or vodka disguised as water? "Yes. A Manhattan, please." I needed something strong. Something that was sophisticated, but trashy enough to get me a good buzz.

"Make that a Greenpoint Manhattan," Alex piped in, boldly making adjustments to my order — "...and tenderloins all around." A step further now, she'd ordered our food, too. Power play much, Alex?

"And for salads?" The waiter looked around to all of us. We were big enough boys to order our greens, I hope.

Big ebony and thick ivory ordered a Caesars. As did I. Alex ordered a virgin salad, whatever the hell that is. Dollars to donuts it has something to do with calories. Eat healthy and then binge on steak. Great diet, Alex.

He didn't write anything down, not even how we liked our steaks. Some rare. Some medium. Some medium-rare. This guy had it all upstairs. My drink order, too, which was A-number-one on my list of priorities. He didn't let me down. In less than a minute he was back with my cocktail. There is a God.

Bitter, potent alcohol hit my tongue, an oasis in this sea of lawyers. Half of the drink was gone before I set the glass down. Too much? Not a chance. Alex was watching though, I could feel it. I think I may have even caught a smile. She must know this is nerve wracking. She's gotta be nervous too, right? Who knows how many glasses of Merlot she pounded before I showed up.

"I'll humor you, Vick. We can skip the casual chitchat and get right to it," Alex said.

I slurped. Here we go. This is what I've been waiting for. How many cups do you need and how many pesos do I get for it, hun? Bring on the bacon.

Alex motioned for one of the attorneys to speak. He pulled out a tablet and slid it to my side of the table. No paperwork this time. Not yet anyway. I read the screen as he talked. "Alexa's doctors have diagnosed your..." Lowering his voice, "...semen, as abbreviated-oxygenation deficient."

Of course, none of that made any sense. Well, the semen part I caught, but the rest sounded like Portuguese. The tablet offered more insight into the diagnosis.

Patient: Victor Miller

Diagnosis: Seminal Abbreviated-Oxygenation Deficiency Syndrome

Description: Patient Miller's semen is absent of oxygenation-conflicting enzymes. Patient's semen dies in .3 seconds when exposed to oxygen, or other common gasses.

Well, that sure makes it difficult to get someone knocked up if my boys die as soon as they're ejected. I set the tablet down on my cloth napkin. "So, you're telling me my semen isn't good anymore?"

"Not exactly, Mr. Miller." The attorney quietly continued, "It doesn't mean your semen is void. It means your semen is non-operational if exposed to open elements."

Alex slammed the rest of her wine. She's barely making eye contact now. I could tell she was getting uncomfortable. "Vick, it means we need to try a different way." She spoke quietly, too.

I can do that. Yeah, I can do that! Thank goodness. I was worried for a second that the cash river had run dry. Kaput. But no! Bring on the dollars, girl. "Okay. That's okay. We'll just try it again." But how? I need to keep my little guys away from air. "I can put them in a condom. That will work, right?" I'm not letting my payday die along with my paratroopers.

The attorneys and Alex were startled by my volume. A few tables looked in my direction. Dangit. I forgot I am in polite company. I lower my voice and they all lean in closely. "That will work, right? They aren't exposed to air that way."

"No..." the plump Caucasian one waved a fat finger. "No, that won't work, Victor. We thought of that. The doctors say the reaction to latex will invalidate the livelihood of the specimen."

That's a hell of a way to say, *rubbers will kill it, too*, Mr. Proper Pants. "Okay... plastic container? Catheter?" Oh man. Did I just say that? The *last* thing I want to do is have a tube shoved up my pecker. Then again for another hundred G's, I'll shove it up there myself.

"Again, we thought of that, Mr. Miller. There is no way to completely rid the tubes of oxygen before inserting it into your..." Even quieter now, "...your penis."

I picked up the tablet and kept reading. There *must* be another way.

> To successfully utilize Donor's (Miller's) specimens, direct, or zero-oxygenation insemination is required for optimal results.
>
> Dr. Gregory Giordonni, MD

Direct insemination? No comprende. Then, as Alex began to speak, it became clear. It hits me like a train full of bricks. I understand why we're out to dinner. I understand why the Olsen twins are here. I knew what she was going to say before she finished her sentence.

"Vick. There is one way this will work." Alex closed her eyes, either of embarrassment or strain. "Penetration. Direct insemination is the only way." She flagged down the waiter for another drink.

I second that.

We waited for our drinks. My attention bounced from the two suits to Alex, back to my empty drink, then back around again. They were waiting for me now. They waited for me to say something, anything that could clue them in to my feelings about this. They weren't alone. I, too, was waiting to see how I felt about this.

It was as confusing as dèjá vu. Maybe there is something I'm missing here. I need to confirm. "Sex? Are you telling me the only way this will work is sex? That is what direct insemination means, right?"

Big White spoke first: "We prefer to call it clinical intercourse."

Our drinks arrived. Alex and I bounced glances to one another while we slurped our booze. Aggressive sips. Nervous gulping is probably the best way to describe it. I probably couldn't have drunk it faster with a funnel.

"It wouldn't be what you're thinking, Mr. Miller." He wiped his brow with a handkerchief.

My glass echoed loudly as I set it down on the table. "Well, then... what am I thinking?"

CHAPTER THIRTY-NINE

My first thought, confusion. That shit's gone now. I understand perfectly what they're looking for. Second, reality. The bottom line? Doctors, attorneys, and Alex all want me to have sex with her instead of letting my boys loose in a cup. Sex. Like, penis in vagina sex. I felt a twitch in my pants. Not now, boy, hush.

Alex sat across the table, peering into her wine with a calm vulnerability. She is a woman in need of something — something precious and personal and intimate. I could hear the crowd around me, forks clacking against plates and humming conversations.

Fat Finger Whitey answered my question. "You're thinking intercourse. The entire act of intercourse." He paused as the waiter filled his water glass. He thanked him and waited for him to leave before he continued. "We don't need the entire act. Just the final moments. Direct insemination at the moment of climax. The rest can..." The waiter returned with bread.

"Is there anything else I can get you while you're waiting for your meal?"

He thanked him and waved him away. "As I was saying, you're thinking of the entire act. Ninety-nine percent of this can be done privately. The last one percent needs to be done clinically."

I've never thought of sex as such a cold process. One percent clinically. Guys, it's still me, sticking my wigwam into Alex and shooting my ... you know. I'm torn. The twenty-year-old me is getting hard. This may be the opportunity of a lifetime, a shag of epic proportions. The reasonable husband (and adult) in me tells me everything is wrong about this situation. *Everything.* No good can come from me fucking her. Sorry, *clinically* fucking her.

I finished my drink. Everyone did. More were on the way, thanks to Alex. Even the attorneys ordered booze this round. It was quiet for a few more minutes. Our eyes passing nervously across the table. Everyone silently contemplating.

Mr. White Lawyer broke the quiet. "Did we mention there is a three hundred thousand dollar contract associated with this procedure?"

CHAPTER FORTY

Three. Hundred. Thousand. United States Dollars. Dineros. Smackeroos. Greenbacks. Stacks. Cheddar. Bags. Three hundred thousand new friends that live in my bank account. Morals leaving your body feels a bit like making deals with the devil. Well, more so deals with the devil's daughter.

I sat back in the leather chair, eating my recently delivered steak. It was rare, bloody, and delicious. Meat melted in my mouth, oozing a salty pleasure on my tongue. It was difficult to concentrate on anything with the racket in my head. I'd created a pro's and con's chalkboard in my brain, mapping both sides of this deal. Big money on one side. Cheating on my wife on the other. The most prominent, circling question: Is it cheating? It's not for pleasure. It isn't because we like each other. I don't even know her.

Is it so different from donating sperm? Same outcome, different procedure. A wee more personal. Alex hadn't said a word in a while. She sat in her chair like a tire with a slow leak. She was buzzed, maybe more than just buzzed. Glossed eyes and a cold smile. What goes on in that brain of yours, Alexa?

They'd showed me the results of an STD panel on the tablet. She is clean. Also, after seeing her half-naked in the hospital gown, I can personally vouch that everything is in order down there.

The lawyers talked quietly to each other. Alex and I remained quiet.

"When do you need this to happen? I'm... I'm not sure about any of this." I finally broke my silence.

Alex spoke. "One, maybe two days, give or take twenty-four hours. That is my most reliable ovulation window."

We sipped our drinks, patted our lips with cloth napkins, and gently pushed pieces of steak into our face holes. The waiter cleared a few plates and dropped a plate of chocolate doo-dads on the table. A pyramid of dessert spheres, drenched in caramel or something rich.

"This is ridiculous, isn't it?" Alex threw her napkin on the table. "I'm sorry, Vick. We're asking too much of you, aren't we?" She turned to her attorneys. "I told you this was a bad idea. I should have listened to my gut, not you." She slammed the rest of her glass of wine. "I think I need to accept that it's not going to happen for me." She stood, thanked me for my time, and walked out of the restaurant.

CHAPTER FORTY-ONE

Alex has a flair for the dramatic, but I didn't think she would leave. "Well, guys. Thank you for your time. Oh, and thank you for dinner." I wanted to confirm that they knew who was paying the bill.

"Mr. Miller…" Cocoa now, taking the lead, "We anticipated a reaction like this. We've been working with Miss Livingston for many years." A stack of paperwork appeared from his leather bag. "It is an emotional subject for her. She tends to…" He glanced to the other attorney, back to me, then adding, "…react hastily."

"Contingency plans, Mr. Miller. We always plan for the worst, and hope for the best with Alexa." The stack fell with a heavy thud on the table. "She is prepared to execute this contract if you are, Mr. Miller."

I flipped a few pages. "I'm not sure, guys." Ice cubes met my lips as I finished the last two fingers of another cocktail. I, too, have consumed a few too many to make sound decisions. "I need some time to think about it."

"In the event you said something like that..." He pulled out a printed page from a folder. "We're willing to adjust the offer to four hundred thousand if you agree in the next twenty-four hours." He slid the page to me. He wasn't kidding. There it is, in printed black ink: *$400,000 for a decision reached in 24 hours or less.*

"I need some time, gentleman. This isn't just donating a..." I made air quotes, "Specimen anymore. This is an affair."

He chuckled. "It is far from an affair, Mr. Miller. An affair insinuates a relationship. There is no relationship. It is business. You have something we need. Supply and demand dictates the price." With a smug expression across his cheeks, he said, "You should adjust your thinking, Mr. Miller."

"I need to digest this. Thanks for the offer."

"Take this with you, Mr. Miller." He handed me the stack and the offer letter. "Please call me if you have any questions or would like to work through this." He took a business card out of his suit jacket and handed it to me.

I pocketed the card, took the offer letter, and slid the heavy contract back across the table. "This time, email the rest to me."

CH4PTER 4OUR2Y-TWO

Daddy didn't know about the helicopter requisition. We can afford it, but it wasn't in the budget. Daddy and his fucking budget. Budget this, and budget that. Fuck your budget, Daddy!

Boom! Boom!

"Alexa! I know you're home..." He is a muffled, screaming voice behind the door.

Boom!

I jump. His fists are pounding harder now. "Nick told me about the helicopter. Do you know how expensive that was? Do you have any idea how much it costs to operate that thing? I have insurance, payments, fuel, flight time, storage fees, flight plans, the pilot's hourly cost, and *his* fucking insurance!" He sighed. A loud, deep sigh echoed through the door. "You can't just take it whenever you need it, Alexa. It's far more expensive than you know. And why are my attorney fees going out of control this quarter? What the hell are you up to, Peanut?"

His shadow is a shifting ghost in the peephole. He pounded again. I am in no mood for his shit today. He is always blubbering on and on about costs, financial decisions, operating costs, blah blah blah blah, blah fucking *blah!* Just once, just this one time, he needs to understand I'm using it for a purpose.

My phone buzzes on a far table. My bare feet along the tile are quiet. He kept pounding. I palm my phone, looking at the screen. He's calling me from outside the door.

"I hear you in there, Alexa. I can hear your phone. I know you're home! C'mon, this is ridiculous. I need to talk with you. You're my daughter for Pete's sake! Please, just let me in."

I let it ring to voicemail. He kept mumbling behind the door. I couldn't understand him. Just talking, then pounding, talking and more knocking.

He waited and I waited. I feather step along the tile once more. Can he hear me walking?

"Peanut? I just want to talk." His voice strained. "Is this about Francis?"

We waited. Neither wanting to speak; both for different reasons.

"Is this some sort of excitement or distraction? Or something else? It's been a tough year or two — you know it, and I know it, but you can't just throw money at these problems. You're going to have to deal with it someday, honey."

He's being nice. That thing he does once in a while to catch me off guard. I can't deal with this today. Too much to do. More planning and more preparation. I'm too busy, can't you see that, Daddy? Do I respond or stay quiet? Do I tell him I'm busy? Or that I was sleeping? Or in the shower?

"If it *is* that, and you're just going through a rough patch..." A cough left his barrel chest. "You need to get control of yourself. I love you, Peanut, always have and always will..."

Tiptoeing again now, quietly, to look through the peephole. Hello, Daddy — I see you. Just to the right of my view I see him, a big, dark blob leaning against the door. What will he say if I let him in? Will it be like last time? Can he keep to his promises?

"Peanut?"

I reached for the knob. The cold metal touched my fingers.

"Peanut. Let me in. Let me *in!* Let me in now! You're spending too much money. What the fuck is your problem? *Stop carrying on about Francis and do your fucking job!*"

He pounded once more. Hard. Everything shook with his final, angry, slamming fist against the door."

"Okay, Peanut. See you in the Rassmusson project meeting next week. In the meantime, stop spending all of our fucking money!"

His dark figure walked away from the door, pushed the button on the elevator, and waited. My eye strained against the peephole. He turned, pierced me with his glare, got onto the elevator, and closed the door.

I slumped to the floor, leaning back against the cold door in my apartment. A tear, the only one I let get the best of me, fell to my shirt. Fucking asshole. You'll see, Daddy. I can show you what real love is. You have no idea. No idea! I can show you why I've spent this money. It wasn't frivolous. It was an investment. The *best* investment. You'll be proud of me when I show you, Daddy.

CHAPTER FORTY-THREE

"Gustavson and Haddock, how can I direct your call?"

"Can you connect me with extension forty-two?"

"Of course, sir. Please hold." Saxophones and pianos played in my ear. Soothing, but still crappy hold music.

"Mr. Miller, I presume?"

It's one of the two attorneys, but I'd jumbled up the cards so I wasn't quite sure which one it was. Didn't matter. The message was the same. "It is. Caller ID?" I asked.

"Yes, sir. I like to see who's calling before I pick up. What can I do for you, Mr. Miller? Are you ready for your next appointment?"

"Actually…" Here it goes. My reluctant, poorly constructed declination. "I can't do it. I just can't bring myself to it. Please send Alex my apologies."

"You can always call her and apologize yourself, Mr. Miller."

"No. No, no. I don't have the stomach for it. I know how much this means to her."

"I understand." A keyboard could be heard in the background. His? Maybe a nearby assistant in the office? "I have one, final offer ready for you, Mr. Miller, in case you were to decline, which you have."

Great. I didn't sleep a wink last night. The idea of passing up nearly half a million dollars for five minutes of fun was a tough enough pill to swallow. It isn't the money though. It's the crime. Regardless of Kraya's condition, I need to stick to my marriage, take the high ground, and walk the moral line to keep myself on the straight and narrow. I don't *need* the money, although it would solve a lot of problems. I have food on the table and a steady income. This would have been gravy. Granted it would have been some delicious, sexy, amazing gravy.

"In the event you decline the previous offer, I am to extend another twenty-four hours."

"I'm going to interrupt you there, Chief. I've decided I can't do it. I don't care."

"Listen, *Chief.* Miss Livingston doesn't take 'no' very well, so please, let me finish my offer. Miss Livingston is prepared to offer you six hundred thousand and an additional one hundred thousand dollar bonus if she is able to become pregnancy positive after the brief interaction."

Seven-friggen-hundred thousand dollars? I think that might make me the highest paid whore in the history of sex. Okay, Vick. Relax here, buddy. You've already made your decision. It's a sin, remember? You can always come back later, but you can't take it back, right?

These fucking morals are getting expensive.

I could retire today and hire a full-time property management company to manage my stuff. Have I become that person? In college, I would have taken three bucks to sleep with her. Hell, maybe would have paid. Today though, I keep telling myself I am a different man. I have a kid. Wife. Family.

"I'm sorry. I cannot accept." I hung up the phone. Will I remember today as the day I made the biggest mistake of my life? My career? Or will I watch this at the pearly gates and get smiles and golf claps from the audience?

CHAPTER FORTY-FOUR

Basement living suits me well. My little guy hangs out with me when I'm home and plays on the floor next to my desk. I'd been sleeping on the futon. Not like the one I had in my twenties either; nowadays they make leather futons with armrests and memory foam and a place for my beer.

I'd done most of my sleeping down here for a few months now. Kraya slept in the attic guest bedroom. There was a bathroom up there and a bunch of her clothes. I hired a rent-a-nurse chick to pop by to check on her a few times a day. She's on seven medications. Seven. Some for depression, some anxiety, some blood pressure, some for who the heck knows.

Our relationship? Strained. I guess strained is a bad word for it — nonexistent maybe? I've gotten better though. More patient. I check on her when I have time, and kiss her forehead when she is sleeping or mumbling to herself. The docs call it dissociated mania disorder. Which, according to the internet, means she's lost her shit.

I catch myself resenting her for it. Really, it's not her fault. If she could, she would be on top of her game. She would be that hot gal I fell in love with. I'm getting good at burying my feelings and caring for her again. I love her, or love the woman she was. In the meantime, I'll care for the dull shell that surrounds my wife. My wonderful, beautiful Kraya. I hope you're still in there somewhere.

She likes to take walks. Sometimes, when she is abnormally aware, she will drive to the store and get some flowers. I wholeheartedly disapprove of her leaving the house, but the babysitter isn't a prison guard. I've found various dings and dents along the front and rear of her car. So many in fact, I struggle to see a spot that is still flush.

It's date night tonight. The night I help her dress up and wear makeup. An evening where the boy is downstairs and we're together in the dining room, trying to make amends with the path that's been presented. Crappy path, but I still need to walk it.

When I came upstairs, she was already waiting at the table sporting a cute flowered dress with her hair pulled back. She looks good. A ball forms in my stomach when I see her looking this way. She looks normal. Like my old Kray.

Vanessa must have helped her tonight. Her lipstick isn't smeared and the shades are blended well. Infinitely better with a woman's touch than my mash-and-glob makeup techniques.

I made her favorite: pasta linguini with chicken. Shredded parmesan on the top and fresh, steamed vegetables on the side. I held her hand and prayed. As the words left my lips, I couldn't help but notice the limp hold of her grip. I push my feelings back into the pit of my chest and whisper the prayer. I need the big man now, like right now, to do something, anything to get me through this. To get *her* through this.

Her dainty fingers try to hold the fork, but she struggles. I lean over and poke a piece of chicken with my fork, and feed it to her. Our eyes meet and for a moment, a brief, magical moment, I see her again. The woman I married. "I love you, Kraya. I'm so sorry I've been distant."

She doesn't respond. She just chews. Her jawline bounces up and down as she chews the chicken. No response, only a million-mile gaze.

I tried a few more times to talk. I'm met with tranquil eyes stammering and tracking me slowly. I ate. Between bites I told her about my day, and the things that had gone on since the last time we had our date night. I talked about the rental houses and that I was thinking about getting her a dog. A puppy was a great idea, I thought. It would give her something to snuggle all day in the attic. She must feel lonely. I can't fill all of these voids; I need to work.

At the end of the night I blew out the candles, put her plate in the sink, and carried her to bed. She'd only fallen asleep a few times during one of my stories tonight. Good times. I could tell she'd lost some weight. She was already a petite thing, even a few pounds made a huge difference. I could feel her spine and ribs as I carried her upstairs. I pulled off her dress, slid on some pajamas, and tucked her into bed. She was snoring before I turned off the light.

I closed her door and sat on the top step. I rubbed the cream-colored carpet and stared up at the ceiling. What is this terrible feeling? Why is my wife so sick? Why is this happening to us? What the fuck? I cursed at the empty stairwell and did something I hadn't done in a long time. I miss Kraya, my wife.

I cried.

CHAPTER FORTY-FIVE

The bar was empty, as it should be at two-thirty in the afternoon. It was dark in there, only the dull orange hanging bulbs above the bar to light up my drink. Jimmy, the bartender, watched the game at the far end of the bar. I stirred my ice cubes with a slim, red straw and took a drink. Vodka is a beautiful thing.

My phone buzzed on the bar. The screen so bright I had to squint to see it. Unknown number.

"Hello?"

"Victor Miller?"

"Yep. What can I do for you?"

"This is Nancy Green, a nurse from Mercy Hospital emergency, your wife has been in an accident." No one can prepare you for those words. The music in the background stopped. The cheers from the game on the TV became blurry. All I could hear was the woman on the phone. I stood, spilling my drink on the bar.

"Oh my gosh, what happened? Is she okay?" I said, frantic now. I can't feel my legs. I'm all out of nerves. I can't decide whether to sit or stand or fall down.

"They are both stable, but your son has some bruising on his face."

My son? What the blooming fuck was she doing driving around with him? "Okay. Okay. Jesus, *okay!* I'll be right down. What room?"

"Emergency two-two-three-A."

I hung up, forgot to pay for my drink, and ran to my car. It took a moment for my eyes to adjust to the daylight. The snow had mostly melted now, replaced with an endless, gray drizzle. Too wet to enjoy the outdoors, too warm to be considered winter.

I felt my phone buzzing in my pocket again, but I didn't get to it in time. I'd had three drinks, but the combination of brightness and alcohol made it difficult to pull out of my parking spot.

After fifteen minutes of one-eyed, blurred driving, I found myself in the parking loop at the hospital. I headed to reception after I parked, asking the obese man in scrubs where I could find *two-two-three-A*. He gave me simple directions, a visitor's badge and buzzed me in. My phone rang again, this time, I answered.

"He-he-hello?" I was out of breath. I didn't realize how fast I'd been running.

"Vick, buddy, I've been trying to reach you." Rob's voice on the line. Surprisingly comforting to hear a friend at a time like this.

"Rob, I'm sorry. Kraya's been in an accident. I am just getting to the ER now."

"I know, Vick. I'm here."

I round the final corner and see Rob on the phone, waiting outside room two-two-three-A. Beside him, my boy, sitting in a wheelchair with a cold pack over his left eye. *Oh, my little guy!* He'd been crying. His wet cheeks as red as a balloon. I knelt, hugging him so tight I thought I might hurt him. "Is he okay? Is she okay?" He hugged me tightly with small, warm arms.

"He's fine, Vick. A bit shaken up, and a bruise here and there, but all the scans are clean. No concussions. No trauma. He's a tough kid." Rob patted him on his tiny shoulder.

"Kraya? Where is she?" My attention turns to Rob now. I'm going to kill her, taking him on a pleasure drive in her condition? She knows better.

"That's why I'm here…"

Rob pointed into the room. I looked at the plaque; it's room two-two-three-A all right. I pop my head in and I'm met with a view of three police officers and a nurse, all talking to Kraya.

"What? What is this? What's going on, Rob?"

A burly officer with a shaved head and tan line shaped like sunglasses turned, saw me, and asked Rob if I am "the husband." He nodded and Big Arms McLaw started asking me questions.

"Is this your wife?" he asked.

I nodded.

"How long has she had a drug problem?" He pulled out a pad and started taking notes.

"He doesn't have to answer that..." Rob injected.

"Look, you're right, he don't need to answer it, but she has a serious problem. I need to know how long she has been on heroin so I can make a recommendation," the police officer said.

"What kind of recommendation?" I asked him, but Rob grabbed my arm and shushed me.

"Treatment or jail..."

Rob pulled me aside, hard enough to hurt my arm. "Dude. Stop talking. They found heroin in the car. *Heroin!* Quite a bit, too." He stopped, looked to his left and right, and whispered, "Did you know?"

"*What*? Heroin? *No, I did not fucking know! This has gotta be a mistake.*"

"No, man. They tested her blood *and* found it in the car. It's heroin."

CH4PTER FO4TY-6IX

The babysitter left for lunch after everyone fell asleep. She usually drives to the bagel shop or to a fast food joint, during which she calls her mother or her pathetic boyfriend. Sometimes she smokes. Sometimes she reads. She is a boring peasant.

I walk through Vick's house with the familiarity of my own. How many times have I been here? Hundreds? Thousands? It's my home away from home. I know every inch. Every magazine and everything in every drawer.

I replace Kraya's pills first. Every few weeks I switch her anxiety medication for a new opiate, narcotic, or psychotropic. This time, a combination of morphine and methylmorphine. Not quite as strong as heroin, but in the same family. Just enough to make her a slug, not enough to kill her. Although I do fantasize about it. One extra milligram and I can end your peasant life. The power I hold, Kraya, you cunt.

Not today though, no, not today. I need to switch them back to her boring anxiety medication. The plan is in motion and everything is set. Just a few more steps. Just a few more, can you believe it? The pill bottle echoes in the bathroom as I shake them into my latex glove.

I use the toilet next, adrenaline usually does that. After I wipe and flush, I move to the boy's room. He is sleeping. He is a sweet boy, like his father. My Vick. Pity he isn't mine. Yet, everything that is Vick's will be mine soon. I will cherish you, young one. I'll hug you and read to you. You'll call me *mother* one day soon, you'll see. You'll forget you even knew your cunt mother. You're going to love it.

His basement man cave is quaint. I smell him on the pillows. I press my face deeply into his futon, inhaling his scent so violently I can taste it. I check his computer for anything new. A few new saved pictures of girls in bikinis and a change to the family budget spreadsheet. Good. Cash is getting tighter with medical bills stacking up. After snooping through a few more rooms, I enter the garage. Kraya's car, parked crookedly as usual, sits in the left stall. I open a small notebook with pictures and notes I'd found online.

The key to cutting brake lines isn't slashing madly, it's gentle and slow. I open the hood and use my fingers to trace the small steel tubes. Where two lines convert to four lines, I make a small mark with a paint pen. The drill is loud, but no one can hear it. Kraya and Vick's son are in dreamland and the babysitter wouldn't return for another 15 minutes.

A red, oil-colored fluid starts to bead from the tiny holes. The goal is to make the holes small enough to be undetectable, but large enough to spit fluid when pressure is applied. As usual, my work is flawless. I hide a small package in the trunk, too. A small, yellow balloon filled with black tar heroin, 2 needles, and a rubber arm strap. The heroin and paraphernalia are nauseating. I'd paid a junkie to find it for me. The needles were the most terrifying. Who knows what lurks in those needles. Drugs? Aids? Bacteria? Vagrants disgust me.

I exit through the side door and pull my blue gloves off with a pop. The trap is set. Now for the bait. The babysitter returns later than I expect, but the plan will still work. When she pulls back into the driveway, her phone is pressed tightly against the side of her head. She rolls down the window, flicks a cigarette butt into Vick's driveway and turns off her engine. Where did she learn this disgusting behavior? Other peasants? Is there some college these people attend to learn how to be proper trailer trash?

I wait for them to finish lunch. My tablet provides me with a crisp video of them around the table, eating in the quiet room. I change views with a swipe and focus on Kraya. I touch her face on the screen. "Your life is about to change, peasant." I smirk. "Time to go…"

I punch her number into my phone. I use a phone number masking app to show the hospital's phone number and caller ID information. I watch as she slowly lifts her head as her cell phone rings.

"Hello?"

"Hi, this is Deputy Farren from the sheriff's department. Your husband had a heart attack and is in the emergency room. He may not have long, so please hurry…"

The peasant perks up. As much as possible anyhow. She grabs her son by his wrist and bolts from the room. The babysitter is shouting now, protesting Kraya's ability to drive. Kraya ignores the sitter, straps the kiddo into the car seat, and flies from the garage.

She passes me on the street. I suddenly realize I easily could have become collateral damage if she lost control and hit my car. Next time I'll be more careful. But there won't be a next time, will there, Kraya? I feel a smile cross my lips.

CHAPTER FORTY-SEVEN

I hope she is sobbing. Bawling so loudly in her cell that her bunkmate punches her. I hope it sucks in jail. I watched them as they dragged her from the hospital bed after she was cleared from medical. Other than a few cuts, she is a picture of good health. Oh, except that she is action-packed with psych issues and addicted to *fuckin' heroin!*

She is in city lockup. I am one phone call away from her bail. I can stop this. I can stop her pain by transferring money to a bail bondsman. A few swipes on an app and a two-minute phone call and she is as free as a bird. Instead, I drink. I drink, and I ponder.

"She'll be fine for the night, buddy," Rob said, comforting me. "I get it. I get why you're mad."

Mad? That's one. Another is rage and hatred and distrust and violation and sadness. A lot of sadness. My wife is on drugs and I didn't know it. I'm so embarrassed that I didn't know. She hid it from me, deciding to live a life of inebriated solitude instead of time with her son and me.

After she was arrested, Rob and I took Junior to the babysitter's place. We needed some time to work through this and a few more cocktails and legal advice was on the menu.

"Thanks for helping, Rob. I'm not mad; *I'm furious*. I-I-I-I can't believe it. I-I-I just... I just can't believe she has been hiding this from me."

"They don't usually come out and say it, dude. People with a problem tend to hide it. Kraya wasn't any different. She was probably scared, man."

"She *should* be scared. You know what this is going to do to her? What it's going to do to *us*?"

"It's not as bad as you're thinking, not the criminal part anyhow. She'll probably do some time in an inpatient treatment ward and be out on probation in a month."

"What's the other part?"

He sighed and took a sip. "She did some pretty heavy damage. A car, a building, signs; the list goes on. You're going to have to pay for it and insurance isn't going to pony up."

"Fuck!"

"Not to mention legal fees."

I glare at him. "Your fees?"

"No, no. I can't take your case on, bud. It's not what I do. Civil is what I'm good at, but I'm not going to do her any favors in criminal court. She'll need someone more qualified. This case might be another hundred thousand. Maybe another fifty for the damage. Treatment cost. Bail, that is, if you ever do decide to bail her out..."

I polish off another drink. That is number five. Or is it six? They can't seem to go down fast enough.

"Don't you think you should take it easy on the booze, bud?"

"It's too much. I can't think." Funny, I *can* think. It's what I'm thinking about that I'm trying to avoid.

"Normal. Totally normal." He drinks more of his beer and shakes his head. "I see clients do this all the time. But take it easy tonight, man. I need you to make some big decisions in the morning." He slides a packet of police and hospital forms across the table. "You need to file these tomorrow morning and bail her out. She can't sit in there forever, Vick. She is your wife after all."

"My wife? I don't even know who she is anymore, Rob." I raised my pointer finger, telling the waiter to pour another drink in bar sign language. He tells me it's my last one by signing back a one-finger throat slit, and fills my glass. "I'll file them tomorrow, don't worry. But I need time to think tonight."

"You want me to pop by Vanessa's to check on your little guy?"

"Please." I can feel the booze now. Not quite strong enough to slur, but strong enough to make the world softer. Thank God.

He takes my hand and shakes it. "I'm sorry. This sucks. It just plain ol' sucks. Sorry this happened to you, buddy."

I nod. "Me, too."

"Take a taxi home, would ya?"

CHAPTER FORTY-EIGHT

Cold rain pitter-pattered on my jacket. I didn't take a cab. Didn't drive either. I needed to walk. I splashed through puddles as I wound through downtown, all while Kraya sat in a cell somewhere, sitting idle in a stale orange jumpsuit. What is going through her head right now? What is she thinking? Better yet, what *was* she thinking?

Cars passed me, spraying waves to the curb. Everyone looked so busy. Some on their phones, others jamming to music. Some drivers spaced out, watching their windshield like a television set. How many others are going through tragedy? How many of these drivers are feeling pain? Probably not many. They all seem so numb and happy, sipping coffee or singing along to the radio.

I'd been walking long enough for my pants to be heavy with rainwater. A neon sign lured me across the sloppy road to the Paddy Whack Tavern, a place that looked as luxurious as a homeless shelter. On the plus side, it had drinks.

Drinks I desperately needed to become as numb as those idiots driving next to me. I bummed a cigarette from a thick, short-haired gal out front. I couldn't tell if she was a motorcycle chick or a lesbian… or both.

I smoked, oh did I ever. She handed me a Marlboro red and half a pack of matches. It'd been too long since I'd had one of those things. My lungs hurt in such a fantastic, familiar burn. I stood outside with her for ten minutes, chatting and laughing under the small awning that shielded us from the rain. She snorted when she laughed, sometimes sending little smoke rings from her mouth. I snubbed my cig and went in after my breath tasted like weed whacker exhaust.

I ordered a bloody Mary, a coffee, and some chicken wings. It was late enough to want dinner now, but there was no way I could go home yet. The bloody tasted good. The chicken did not; all rubber wings and strings. The coffee was gross, too, but no one is showing up to this tavern to drink coffee. I slurped the bloody and looked at the police documents. I read the initial report and the drug analysis. It said she "appeared to be intoxicated as she was pulled from the vehicle. Further medical tests proved she was under the influence of heroin…" They also found "…a tarry substance consistent with the smell, texture, and feel of heroin in the trunk. Field tests confirm heroin. Needles. A tie-off tourniquet." Geez! It's all here. It's been happening right under my nose.

I set the police packet on the battered wooden table and moved farther into the stack of documents. Next I see photos of the damage. A building, light pole, parked car, and a mailbox were all in her path. None survived. The report estimated four hundred thousand in damages, but that was some cop's estimate. Rob told me they usually ballpark it. Farther into the stack was a letter from child services. Fuck, I never considered CPS. I read. Yadda, yadda, yadda, drugs in home, blah blah, we need to perform a home inspection to evaluate the safety of your child/children, yadda, blah, yadda. The rabbit hole just kept getting deeper.

I finished my bloody Mary and asked my waitress for another. My friendly waitress asked, "What are way celebratin'?" with a sweet Southern drawl unnatural to hear this far north. I just smile like an idiot. Despite my silence, she smiled back and told me she'd be "rot back" with my drink. I hope so.

I flipped to another set of pages from the DMV. A license forfeiture form and demand for insurance were at the top of that stack. "Kraya Louise Miller, your license has been hereby revoked by the state of Minnesota and will remain suspended until your hearing. If you have any questions, contact, blah, blah, blah."

I pressed my fingers to my temples and closed my eyes.

Buzz! I didn't look. Instead I grabbed my fresh bloody Mary and took three monster gulps. Who was texting me? Who was texting me *tonight*? Of all nights? I check my phone. Alexa Livingston. Awesome. Just what I need right now.

"Let's chat."

I typed back: "I'm in the middle of something, Alex. I'll call you next week." Another bite from the basket of wings. Yep, just as disgusting as the last.

Buzz!

"It's been months since we've talked. I'd like to make you another offer."

I sipped my gross coffee and typed back: "It's a bad time."

Almost immediately. *Buzz!*

It read, "$650,000."

Nothing more in the text, just that number. The screen is blurry. I need more coffee, pronto. I was *just* starting to enjoy my buzz, too. I slapped myself and told the waitress to get me three glasses of water and another coffee. I have work to do, and Alex isn't helping.

"Let's talk next week, Alex." I can't dedicate any extra brain cells to this right now.

Then came: "$750,000"

Again, just a number. I wondered how much more I could tick up this dollar amount. Can I get her to a million?

"Final offer, Vick."

That answers *that* question. I flipped the pages back to the damages sheet. It's going to be expensive, Kraya. Why did you do this?

Seven hundred fifty thousand dollars. It's even a lot of words. Seven. Hundred. Fifty. *Thousand.* Dollars. I'll need at least four or five hundred thousand just to get through this mess.

"Final offer. Valid for twenty-four hours."

CHAPTER FOU4TY-9I9E

The red dot moves on the map. Vick is a few blocks from me — how exiting! He stopped at that shithole saloon on Fourth. Poor Vick. What a day. I'll take care of you. *Let me take care of you!* I bet you've had a lot to drink, too. My poor baby is *soooooo* stressed.

Now, Alex, this is it. Send the offer. I'm so excited I can barely see. I type "Final offer. Valid for 24 hours." It isn't about the money. It's about timing. He needs something right now. He needs someone to be there for him. My body is that conduit. Me, Vick! *Me!*

I pace the apartment — 5 seconds go by — 10, then 20. A full minute has passed without a response. I check the computer and see that he is still at the bar in the same seat. The glowing dot hasn't wavered; it mocks me, blinking at me, telling me *no*.

"C'mon, honey. *Respond*, please..." I'm a wreck — 5 minutes pass. Is he ignoring me? Waiting — 20 minutes. *Really, Vick? Really?* I can give you so much! I can be perfect for you! *Give in to your needs, Vick!* I can make your problems go away!

Buzz!

He responds: "Let's talk."

This is it. This is *really* it! Stop. Play it cool. Stop *fidgeting*. Cool, Alex, cool. I respond: "My office?"

He responds: "I can't now, how about tomorrow morning? Say, ten a.m.?"

Why are you stalling, Vick? Why are you putting this off? It's inevitable. It's perfect. It's us! Ha! This is *so* us. "That time isn't good for me. I'm free in about half an hour for 10 minutes. Then I have meetings all night and tomorrow morning."

Tick tock. I can't believe it. Vick, do you have any idea how exciting this is? Do you know how long I've been working to create this path? The end of the road and the beginning of a new, beautiful journey together. *Stop fidgeting!*

No response. Nothing. Another 5 agonizing minutes pass before I see anything. But not a text, a blink. The blinking red dot moves and my heart rate skyrockets. The phone is inches from my nose now.

Where are you going, Professor? I see you.

"Okay," Vick finally says back.

I cheer so loudly my walls cheer back. My heart is prancing! I can't believe it. He is coming here. *Coming here!* It worked! I'm not much of a dancer when I'm alone, but I feel my feet frolicking and my arms flailing. Wait. *Stop!* I need to get ready. Not a moment to lose.

I rush to the bathroom, feet skidding to a halt before the sink. Drawers fly open. *There it is!* I grab the bottle of douche and leap into the shower. Cold water, then hot. It feels amazing on my skin. This is how it feels to win. I always win! My Vick. He is coming. I fill the tiny bottle with water and slip it in. I squeeze the bulb and water sprays inside me.

I repeat the process a few times and shave the important parts. Slowly, the razor traces my pubic bone. I need to relax. Breathe. If I cut myself I won't be perfect. Breathe. Shave. Exhale. Shave. Rinse. I hit my armpits, too, but carefully. They've healed well, but they're a bit uneven and asking for a nick from my razor. After I finish shaving I rub vanilla body wash everywhere, careful not to wet my hair.

My right foot slips as I exit the shower and I catch myself. *Slow down, Alex,* this is crunch time. Too much time preparing to let something happen now. Watch your footsteps; count backward from 10.

I wipe my shoulders first, then breasts and pits. My stomach, crotch, and thighs next. Lotion pumps frantically from a gold-colored bottle into my palm. I spread it evenly along every crevice of my body. I spray perfume in the air, and walk through it as it gently drifts to the floor.

Dry shampoo creates a small cloud of particles, enough to make my hair shine. Flyaways are my enemy tonight. I enter room 9, naked and still dripping. I pat myself dry and slide into the special red dress I keep hung up in the corner. I picked it out for this occasion, the day I own my Vick. The day he comes to me. Tonight, he will be mine.

It's smooth on my skin. Goosebumps speckle my arms and legs. I zip the back and climb into a pair of stockings and tall pumps. I fasten the garter belt and slither into a clean pair of panties. I skip the bra because I've kept them perky enough to pull this off.

A light necklace crosses my collarbone, secured in the back with a snap. I gargle, brush my teeth, and run a brush through my hair. It catches my eye. At first I think it's a shadow, a reflection. No. *No!* A blemish on my cheek! A zit, making its way to the surface. Fuck. *Fuck!* It's hideous. What am I going to do? I'm a *monster!*

Breathe. Stop. *Stop fidgeting* and follow the plan. It's almost done. Fix your makeup and cover up that blasphemous thing. Stick to the plan, honey. I inhale, close my eyes, and exhale. Again and again, breathing in smooth repetition. Yes. *Yes*. This is it. I grab my concealer and slide the brush across my cheek.

It's been 11 minutes. He'll be here soon. He is a blinking blip on Walnut Avenue now. Maybe 5 minutes away? Much to do. I sing it! *Much to do!*

I pull the sheets tight on the bed and pick up scattered laundry from the floor. It is already quite clean, but I need perfection tonight. Nothing but the best for my professor. Wine. I need wine, too. The cork pops from a bottle of 1995 Merlot and the fine red pours into my glass. I need this. Smooth flavor runs down my throat. Amazing. Absolutely amazing how one drink can calm my nerves. Not completely, but enough to breathe easier.

The red dot approaches. He is nearing the building now. What remains? What steps do I need to finish before... before... before he is *here!* Just one.

I snag my phone and text him: "I'm running late, Vick. Please stop by my apartment on the 44th floor. I only have a few minutes."

Beautiful. Perfect! I've recited this text hundreds of times. The perfect combination of words to create a sense of urgency without being overly aggressive.

Come to me.

CHAPTER FIFTY

I'm soaked. It doesn't matter. Fuck it, nothing matters today. Kraya's in jail and my kid was almost killed by his bitch of a mother. The booze now running rampant in my veins — angry blood pumps through me.

Can I negotiate something else with Alexa Livingston, at least until I get a divorce? Pfft, I'm sure. She's a sucker for my swimmers. Maybe I can get another few hundred G's for another sample. I laugh, "Sample! Ha!" What a joke.

Livingston Tower is huge. Holy shit it's big. My neck cranes as I take in the sight of the building. Hundreds of tiny offices and apartments, some with lights on, some off. Rain blasts my eyes. I'm not even wiping it off anymore, it's a waste of time. New clothes, warmth, and a towel are the only things that can fix this depth of sogginess. I reach the front desk and a handsome Asian chick looks back at me.

"I have an appointment with Alexa. Alexa Livingston."

"Mr. Miller? Of course. Go ahead, I'll buzz you in."

No escort this time. No butler. Everyone must have gone home for the day. No bother, I think I'm getting the hang of this place. I sway past the big reception area and find the elevators after a few wrong turns. I push the button and a voice squeaks over the intercom. "I'll clear you now, Mr. Miller. Thank you."

The elevator roars to life from some floor above. It takes a few seconds, but eventually it picks me up. Man those bloody Marys were good. I should go there again. What was it called? Crazy Pete's, or something? Whatever.

The heavy golden doors open into Alex's hallway. I'm feeling out of place. It is so clean, so nice in here and I'm soaked, drunk, and here to try to weasel another boatload of cash from the owner's daughter. Maybe I didn't think this through. Nah, I'm here. Maybe she'll be... Alex opens her apartment door, revealing a red dress and a pair of legs.

"Vick."

"Alex. Wow. It's, umm, nice to see you, too. I wanted to…"

"I only have a few minutes, Professor, please come in. Quickly now. We should talk."

She shows me in. As usual, it's cleaner than a surgical room. Her bedroom door is open, same as her office. The closet with the six on the door and the storage room are both closed. There is red wine on the table and a plate of half-eaten cheese and crackers.

"Come in, come in." She pauses, troubled. "My God, Professor, you're soaked!"

"Yeah, it's a long story." I wonder what I must smell like.

"You must be freezing!" She looks worried, frantic even. Like a mother concerned about her pup with the flu. She whisks into the bathroom and reappears with a thick towel. She wraps it around me. It's warm and feels softer than any towel I'd ever touched.

"Thank you. This is wonderful." I pull the towel tightly against my body. She grabs an empty glass and fills it with wine. She tilts the bottle in my direction and offers it to me. I happily accept. Why not? I'm not driving.

"Have you accepted my offer, Vick?" She sits on a stool with her legs spread ever so slightly, revealing the tip of a shadowed lace garter set.

"I want to discuss our previous arrangement. I'm not comfortable with…" She stopped me by raising a hand in the air. She clapped her legs together and stood.

"Vick. I don't ever want to do anything you aren't comfortable with." Her hand moves to my cheek. Was she always this touchy-feely? Or am I hammered?

"Yeah, about that…"

Drunk or not, I remember that she has a fetish for interruption. She places her finger to my lips. "Shhhh, Vick…" Her finger slides from my lips to my chin and continues to my hand. "What are you comfortable with, Vick? Your feelings are number one."

"I'm willing to give it another shot, but not…" I raise a pair of fingers into air-quotes — "*directly*. It… it feels wrong. I'm married, and I think…"

Her lips stop everything. Fluffy pillows of sensuality against me. My eyes widen and I feel the burning desire to rip her clothes off and fuck her on the counter. Not for a stupid sample, but to satisfy this drunken lust. The angel and devil on my shoulder are arguing again. Her tongue slips between my teeth. Delicate and moist, it dances and flicks. My groin stiffens against my wet boxers.

The angel wins and he is just as surprised as I am. I push her back, snapping us from this trance. Alex blinks, confused and a bit disappointed. I wipe her from my lips with a wet sleeve.

"I'm sorry, Alex. I… I can't do this."

I need to leave. Holy shit, do I ever. This has become something it shouldn't. It's gone too far. What am I doing? Fuck! Wait, what was *she* doing? I need to leave. This is... this is... it's too much to handle. I need to deal with Kraya before I go off and start an affair with the rich girl next-door. Oh shit. Kraya! I almost forgot she's sitting in a cell somewhere. Before you start feeling all sad, remember she almost killed your son, dude, remember? Fuck. *Fuck.* I remember now. I need more booze. I need to leave, and I need more booze.

No words, I turn to head toward the door. We can discuss this another day. A warmer, less rainy, sober day. I hear it then. A high-pitched squealing sound that tears into my guts. I feel it in the deepest pit of my stomach. I hate this sound.

I turn to Alex who's sagged herself over the counter, crying into a napkin. She pauses, slams the wine, takes a few rushed, double breaths, and cries again.

"Go. Just... just go!" she's yelling from behind a napkin. Mascara streaming down her cheeks.

"I'm so sorry. It's not you. Really. I just can't do it. I'm still married," I say as I point to my ring.

She looks up from her slouch. "I've put so much pressure on you. (Sniffle) Hell, I put too much pressure on me. I wanted that baby so bad..." She cries again. My feet carry me to her without thinking. I wrap a consoling arm around her and try to hug her pain away.

"Just go, Vick. It's never going to happen for me. I need to accept it!"

Warm tears melt into my wet shirt. I hold her tightly. Her back rises and falls with stuttered, sobbing breaths. I push her head into my neck and I whisper, "It's all going to be okay, Alex. I'm not going anywhere yet. It's not over. I can try again as many times as it takes..." A woman's cry is my Achilles heel, my kryptonite. Fuckin' sucks when the tear train starts thundering down the line.

"You'll keep trying?" Vulnerable, wet eyes emerge. She looks young. Innocent. Something I hadn't seen in her. She wipes her cheek, smudging a long line of makeup across her face.

"Of course I'll keep helping..." Please stop crying. For fucks sake, woman, please stop crying. I pull her closer, partly because I'm a nice guy, and mostly because I can feel her warmth through these cold-ass clothes. Her head, just moments ago buried in my chest, glides slowly to my face. She's smiling, with glistening cheeks and innocence in her eyes as she pushes her lips into mine again.

CHAPTER FIFTY-ONE

Soft lips join. It's deliberate and gentle. It feels good to feel something. I'll stop it, I *need* to stop it. But not yet. Not *quite* yet. It feels good and I haven't felt this good in a long time. We didn't move, our lips frozen together. I feel a warm tear drop from her nose to my cheek.

My marriage is in shambles. What else do I have to lose? *Fuck it.*

Her petite frame is light and easy to grip. I wrap my hand around her neck, pulling her mouth into mine. Sliding tongues slither and play as aggressive fingertips scratched my skin. I slid my hands down her back, skin mesmerizingly taut and smooth.

My mind is busy — *What are you doing? Whoa, hold on, cowboy! I need to stop this before it goes too far!* I pull back and our eyes flicker. Her hand wraps around my wrist, guiding it between her legs through the spread of her dress. Radiating heat and silk panties meet my palm.

My mouth parts, eyes widen. I couldn't think straight. My finger pauses and quivers on the wet lips behind her panties. Seizing the opportunity, Alex slides her tongue back into my open mouth and uses her left hand to slip her panties to the side.

Slick, warm folds grip my finger as it glides inside her. I'm out of focus, in a dream I can't control. Too many lonely nights and fantasies, fantasies about her. I feel myself harden as she grabs my bulge from outside my pants. Her slit pulses on my finger as it slides in and out. She stands unexpectedly, popping my wet finger from inside her.

She takes a gentle step back, beaming. A tan, fragile arm slides the strap of her dress from a delicate shoulder. The dress slinks to the floor with a hushed thud. Her hand on mine again, dragging me into the bedroom.

I should stop, it's not too late. C'mon! Wake up, dude! You need to... I slump to the bed and she is on me, sitting on my lap before I can make an objection. An objection I wanted to make so badly that I said nothing. I feel writhing against my groin, sliding her smooth panties back and forth on my pants. My hands cup her breasts and she gently nibbles my ear.

My zipper slips down, replaced with a slithering hand. Skin and fingers slide tenderly on my bare shaft. Rhythmic palms sliding, up and down my guy. Alex whispers in my ear. I can't hear her, but I can feel her breath.

She kisses me again. More tongue. More aggressive. She pulls my sticky, wet shirt from my back. Chills along my skin as the cool air hits the moisture. Her breasts meet my mine and heat blossoms from tits to chest.

I kissed her back, slipping her the sloppy drunk passion I'd been craving for too many nights. She's making little noises now. Those sexy, high-pitched noises that erupt involuntarily when you flick a nipple or suck on a finger in just the right way. Angry legs see-saw my pants from side to side, finally freeing them from my waistline. Wet boxers slide down my legs. I follow, yanking her panties past her thighs. Small, dainty, stretchy things that flick off in a snap.

She's above me, draping shoots of hair on my face. Her hand still gripping my girth, aims me into position. She lifts herself and presses her gap against me. I enter, but just the tip. A smooth, tight pleasure from the tippy-top. She lifts herself again and slides back down — more this time. She is silky and snug and keeps pressing farther. Past my head now, she kisses me, lifting her waist and pushing back down again. Her elastic grips me like a fist. I plunge the last piece of me into her wetness.

Pressure is building. Her breasts are bouncing slowly with the rise and fall of her body. I close my eyes. Smells of sex and perfume fill my nose. We're inside each other, her tongue in my mouth, my dick buried inside her.

I focus on the rhythmic pleasure, her creamy padding cradling my prick. Up and down. Back and forth. More pressure is building. I'm getting closer. Her lips touch my ear again. I can hear the whisper this time. She's almost there. She rocks faster, grinding against my pelvis. Throbbing, I clench my fists and hold myself back for another few moments until I hear her say those two, magical words again. She screams it, digging fingernails into my chest. "I'm cumming!"

I erupt into pleasure as her walls clench around me. We tighten, holding each other closely as our bodies burst and spasm. Moaning — some mine, some hers. I feel her dripping down my shaft as the sweeping endorphins and sparks begin to fade.

Exhausted and quivering, she falls to my chest. I feel her breathing against my stomach. I'm out of breath, too. We're slick with sweat and wet. The apartment is quiet again. I hear only our heavy breathing and a few sirens in the distance.

CHAPTER FIFTY-TWO

My phone buzzed from somewhere nearby. I grabbed for it, but miss the table. I tried again, waving my hand blindly to find the damn thing with no avail. I opened one eye and realized the table is not there. Nor was I sleeping on my futon. Both eyes open then, revealing the serene bedroom of Alexa Livingston.

Hole-leeeeeee shit. Memories flash and suddenly I remembered everything from last night. Kraya. The accident. Heroin. The bars. The booze. More booze. Even more booze, and then... Fuck!

I sat up to find I was still naked under the fluffy white comforter and assault of endless pillows. Alex was nowhere to be found, thank God. I wouldn't know what to say. I grabbed my phone from a side table that was farther away and taller than mine at home. I unlocked the screen and found several new messages.

Text message from Rob: "Hey, dude. I checked on Junior for you. He's fine. He is going to stay with your sitter."

Next text message from Rob: "What happened to you last night?"

Yet another text message from Rob: "Yo! Call me when you can. We still need to get bail figured out, like, this morning."

I swiped them away and checked for other messages. Nothing important. I found nothing but a headache that won't quit and a full bladder. My clothes were nowhere to be found — awesome. I found a bath towel on the floor that was probably used to clean up God-knows-what, wrapped it around my waist, and started exploring. I pushed her bedroom door open slowly and saw a narrow table sitting outside the door. On the table: a stack of clothes and an envelope, next to a thermos and a bottle of water. I opened the envelope.

Vick... What a wonderful night! Don't worry, our secret is safe. I washed and dried your clothes and made you some coffee. I had some early meetings today, so I won't be back until lunch. Please, make yourself at home. If the coffee isn't hot please make more. Oh, and take these with a full bottle of water right away to beat back a hangover. - Alex

I poured two pills from the envelope and popped them in my mouth, then drowned them with the lukewarm coffee from the thermos. A check fell from the envelope, too.

A check written to me for seven hundred and fifty thousand dollars in curly blue handwriting. I forgot about my headache. I lost my thoughts about Kraya and bail and Rob and the cum-stained towel. I forgot about sex with the heiress and misplaced my concern about my son for a full minute.

I've never held this much money. Well, I've never held this much of *my own money* anyway. My legal issues with Kraya are solved. Business will grow again and I'll be able to afford a divorce and a nice settlement from my deranged, heroin-addicted liar of a wife. *Oh, Kraya, how did this happen?* I dropped my towel in Alexa's living room and slid into my clean clothes. Judging by the yellow, stapled tag on the buttonhole, they'd been dry cleaned.

The coffee is cold so I take her advice and brew another pot. I sit at the bar while it brews, fixated on the check. A few pictures catch my eye, too. My weird mirrored clone, her ex-husband, stares back at me from a far wall with a goofy familiar grin. I checked out a few more photos on an adjacent wall. Alexa hugging him by the Leaning Tower. Another one laughing at a restaurant. We're everywhere.

I don't feel regret about last night, not at all. There is something there though, some dread hiding in that warm spot in my stomach. Or maybe it's that I regret *not* feeling regret. I poured out my old, cold coffee and replaced it with the new stuff. It's piping hot and delicious. Gourmet hazelnut or something. I bet it's more per gram than cocaine.

I continued my tour of her place, looking at my doppelganger as I stroll. It's an absolute mind fuck. I can't stop snooping, walking room to room, looking at this dude. Here is one of him at the mall, laughing. Another with her at a museum. One over there at a pool, drinking martinis. He's in good shape, which is nice because I'm complimenting a mirror. His swim trunks even look designer. I wonder how rich this guy was. I wondered... waited. What is that?

I catch something. I pulled a frame from the wall, the nail dropping to the floor as a noisy casualty. I brushed the glass with my fingers and slid the picture under a nearby lamp. What the frig is this? No. It... it can't be. I set it down under the light, quickly going back to the picture of the two of them at the ocean, yanking it from the wall, too. I placed them side by side under the lamp.

My mug shattered on the tile. I'm shaking. He has my scar. *My scar?* How is this possible? My bullet wound in one photo, concealed poorly in the other. I stuffed the check into my pocket and ran for the door, opened it, jogged through it, and slammed it hard enough to echo. I repeatedly pressed the elevator *call* button. *Click, click, click, click, click —* C'mon, *c'mon!*

The photo of Francis has a scar on his shoulder, the other picture does not. Instead, it has a blurred circle over the shoulder, blended well enough to be mostly unnoticeable. Those images aren't her ex-husband. They are photos of me.

C5APT5R FI5TY-THR33

He's beautiful when he sleeps. I couldn't sleep a wink, not for even a moment. I lay there all night, watching the rise and fall of his chest with the smell of our sex still fresh in his pores. The things I've never noticed about him make him even more perfect now. I knew he mumbled in his sleep, but I never knew what he was saying. I'm able to lean in, ear nearly touching his blissful lips, and listen to his hushed, precious voice as he speaks.

I counted the curly hairs in his armpit and pressed my body against his for hours. I figured he would wake up around eight or eight-thirty, his normal schedule, so I made coffee and a care package for him when he woke. It took a lot of willpower to leave him.

I wait now, in room 9. I watch him in my room from the cameras and monitors. I watched him sleep and now I'm blessed to watch him start to wake up. Invigorating! Exciting! What a thrill! Yet pieces of the plan still remain. Focus on the prize.

I should shower, but the thought of evacuating his seed is a felony. His sweat and fluids are still on me and inside me. I don't think I'll ever shower again. Will I ever shower again? Seriously, can I bring myself to wipe him from my orifices and skin? Shit, I didn't think this part through. How can I ever get clean again and keep his scent fresh on my skin? Focus... focus.

He's awake now, enjoying his coffee in my apartment. This is the way it should be. He should wake up *here* every day. He looks happy and content. He looks like he is in love. After last night, I can't imagine he isn't! The check is a nice touch, too. I need to keep him happy, and keep him on his toes. I need him to associate my body with pleasure and wealth and happiness. The plan is working. I'm rewiring his mind. Soon, love, soon you'll be mine forever, just like we planned.

What is this feeling in my tummy? How can I feel off when my Vick is walking around the apartment? Snooping is such a terrible word, especially when you love someone. Is learning a better word? Yes. He is learning more about me through my possessions. Perhaps he's nesting and making himself at home. Is he making plans to marry me and spend a life here?

What are you doing now, my curious bunny? What could you possibly be doing taking that picture off the wall? He *must* be looking at my bikini. I picked that swimsuit just for you, love. I picked that one over the green and gold one-piece they told me looked "fabulous." I hope you enjoy it... Wait, what's wrong, honey? What are you doing?

The video feed from just outside the door shows him pacing, angrily looking back and forth between photos. What is it, baby? What is wrong? His coffee hits the floor. *Shit, shit, shit!* I want to leave this room so badly and hug him and kiss him and snuggle him and hold him and tell him it's okay, whatever it is, it's going to be fine! My heart explodes with irregular beats.

He bolts from sight. I follow him on the cameras to the elevator. He's leaving? Where is he going? I need to know!

I unlock room 9 from the inside and run to the elevator. I see a collapsing orange light as the doors squeeze shut. *Damn!* I didn't catch him! I push the *call* button frantically and I wait. And I wait. I wait for-fucking-ever! Where is he going? I grab my phone and open the tracking app. It says he is in the apartment. Shit, did he leave his phone?

Finally, the elevator door opens and I hustle in, blasting the button with a painted pointer. I need to get to my car on the third floor garage before he leaves. I need to follow him using his car's GPS, not his phone. Damn, what is it?

CHAPTER FIFTY-FOUR

Why would she have doctored images of me in her apartment? It's too much for my hungover mind to decode this early in the morning. Before I decode this Alexa-picture-shit-storm thing, I needed to check in with Rob and the babysitter. It's going to be a busy morning trying to figure out what to do with my jailbird wife.

After patting my pocket I realized it was empty. Like a panicked ninja I checked my other pockets. Nothing. *Shit, I left it at her place.* I turned back down the hall and caught the next elevator up. It's busy, but it eventually lands and picks me up. I press her floor and enter one-one-three-zero. Jackpot! She hasn't changed it. Will I ever have to explain why I broke a coffee mug on her floor and left?

The aroma of naked bodies, coffee, and ass lingered. I jogged down the hall to her bedroom and retrieved the phone.

As I reached the front door, something caught my eye. The small room, off to the side, was open. It'd never been open. I paused midstride, hand still on the doorknob. I let go and walked to the door with the number six on the face and opened it wider. There wasn't a ray of natural light in there, so my eyes took a moment to adjust. My fingers fumbled to find the light switch to flick it on.

Countless screens were mounted on the far wall. Every one of 'em showing a different view on split screens. It looked like a bizarre, cluttered command center. I cocked my head and recognized what they were watching. *My* house. *My* garage. *My* bathroom. Everything. Literally, every perceivable view in my home was under surveillance from this odd little room. I snagged one of many mice on the desk to navigate through the camera screens. My rentals were bugged, too. She'd been watching my tenants?

My hands trembled and I dropped the mouse. The opposing wall covered, floor to ceiling, with photos. Images of me. Pictures of me walking across the street, laughing, sleeping, in class, in high school, at the gym. Naked. Clothed. Hundreds of pictures. Others, too, with Kraya, crossed off with a manic, hand-carved X on her face. Many dozens, maybe even one hundred or so.

A mannequin stood bearing a printout of my face taped crudely to his head. My old leather jacket, watch, and t-shirt slung on his plastic body. The Rolex she gave me was there, too. A collection of my old drivers licenses, handwritten notes, condoms, and other things I recognized were also there, brightly lit in cases on pedestals. These are mine. All of these things are mine. I sold these online last year. *Alexa fucking bought them.*

A few chairs and a mattress were in there, too, tucked in a corner next to a table. The bed had stained, shiny sheets and the chairs were adorned with slashes and burn marks. On the table, dildos. Too many to count. Big ones, small ones, black, red, and white. Next to the box of dicks was a box of medications. Drugs in various orange bottles. Creams, pills, liquids, and sprays. Painkillers and antidepressants and stimulants, oh my. I picked up a familiar-looking dial of pills and opened it. A prescription pill pack for birth control. Every day missing from the circular dial except yesterday and today. I flip it over and see Alexa's name on the package.

I'm lightheaded. I've gotta get out of here. I looked at the monitors one final time on my way out. On the far screen I saw someone. Someone standing. No, no, not standing, waiting. Someone is waiting with crossed arms. Where is it? A rental? No. It's not. It's not my rental property or my home. I recognize it now. It's Alexa. Alexa Livingston is standing outside this very room.

She is waiting for me.

CHAPTER FIFTY-FIVE

"We should talk, Professor," Alex says.

"You don't need to explain, Alex. I'm going to leave and pretend I, ah… pretend I never saw any of this." I feel like someone is turning down the lights in my skull. *I need to get the fuck out of here.* Who are you, Alexa? Who the fuck are you? What is that shrine room of yours? My legs wobble as I walk, backing away from her into the kitchen.

"It's not that simple now, Vick."

She smiles and tells me to sit down. That she'll explain it all to me. I move through the kitchen and I grab the biggest, baddest knife from her block and hold it out. "Something is wrong with you, Alex. Something is wrong. You need help, Alex!"

"Help? Like a therapist? Ha! Don't *ever* tell me to see her again — honey." A short burst of unexpected laughter mid-sentence — "…sorry, love. But that hurts my feelings."

I shake my head, not to agree, but because it's clear she's a few sheets shy of a ream.

"Put that down and let's talk," Alex said, pointing to the counter.

Nope. Not happening. I walk behind her, making my dash to the door. She isn't scared, not in the least.

"I'll fuckin' stab you if you get closer, Alex. I'm serious. I'm leaving…"

"Oh, come now, Professor…" She shifts in front of me and got closer, and closer, and closer with that smile. "We have *so* much to talk about."

Smiling. Always smiling…

C5APTE6 5IFTY-6IX

I was able to grab the knife but he fell too fast and too hard for me to break his fall. I feel awful. His head hit the ground so hard when I tazed him. Do you know how hard I've worked for this? Do you? *Do you, Vick*? Stop fidgeting. Stop. *Stop this*. The plan is fucked! *Fucked!* Maybe not. Maybe I can fix this. Stop fidgeting. He is right here! The one you've tried *so* hard to get is in front of you... and you're telling me the plan is fucked? What are you talking about? It's perfect.

I am strong enough to drag him to the bed and tend to the bump on his head. Thank goodness for Pilates and leg workouts. "I'm here now, honey. Shhhhhh. I'm here. You'll wake up and be all better." I use ice packs and bandages to keep the swelling down.

His veins are perfect for needles. I bounce my finger on a big juicy one in his forearm and plunge the needle into his vein. It's only morphine, just enough to make him feel better —happier and more relaxed, too. Just what he needs right now.

It took 20 minutes for him to wake up. His eyes aren't scared and alert anymore. They're soft and gentle, like his mind. Good, Vick. Enjoy the drugs. It'll make you feel all better.

"Whaaa… what happened?" he said.

"You fell. All the excitement maybe? You were quite flustered."

"I was? Wait… I remem… what are you doing to me?" He pulls against the restraints on his arms and legs. I used common hospital restraints, the light brown leather type. I ordered them years ago for a different purpose. They're working just as well as they did then. Good as new.

"Shhh, Vick, relax," I said. "You need rest."

"How can I fucking relax when I'm tied to your bed? What are you doing?" He flails uselessly with the look of panic on his brow again. It's painful to see someone you love like this.

"Victor Miller, calm down…" Why am I scolding him? My love, forgive me? "You'll need more if we're going to have a civil conversation." I pop off the syringe cap with my teeth. He squirms a bit, but I find a vein easily enough. I push more juice into his bloodstream. Whipping, anxious arms slow and his eyes squint. He's stoned, calm, and cool. "All right now, Vick. We need to talk. Don't you agree?"

"Ummm, yeah. Mmmmgmmm."

I feel happiness creeping along the folds of my face. Good — he's conscious and can speak, but has the mumbles, a sure sign he's had enough of this stuff. I set down the needle and slide it back into the drawer.

"Vick? Baby... You know almost everything now." I tilt my head shyly. "It's early, but we'll make do. You weren't supposed to find out like this. It was supposed to be different. But. *But!* We can improvise, can't we?" He nods. He closes his eyes for a moment and reopens them.

"We... well..." I pause. I can't believe the time has come. We're here! "I'll just say it. We're meant to be together, Vick! The sun and the moon, the gods, everything points to us being together. Every fabric of my being is drawn to you. It's the highest form of flattery, you know?"

"Mmm — flattered," Vick says.

He blinks. Was that sarcasm? You're so funny! "You have a few options, Vick. One, go back to your normal life. Pretend like this never happened, or..." I can hardly contain the glee and anticipation. "...you can choose to be with *me*. You've shared my body and we have secrets and trust. We're perfect, Vick."

"I donn... I dunno though. I... I... I wanna... mmmgmmm."

"What do you need? What do you want to know? I'm all yours."

"Everythinggg else..." He smiled. "...and lemme free."

Was that the drugs? Or is he seeing things clearly now. He is seeing me clearly. He must. Holy hell, he is coming around. "Everything else? Can you be specific?"

Vick passed out. My sweet, sweet sleepyhead. I sing to him and pet his forehead. "Twinkle twinkle little star, how I wonder what you are."

Don't worry, honey. I'll be here when you wake up.

CHAPTER FIFTY-SEVEN

When I open my eyes, Alex is lying next to me, grinning ear to ear. I feel like I'm the butt end of a shitty joke and… I'm foggy — forgetful maybe. Dammit, I remember now. She dosed me. It's a struggle to stay in reality. My mind drifts back and forth, to and from the room, from the bed, into the clouds and back to the bed again. Fucking drugs. I can't tell if it's amazing or terrifying. Maybe both? Definitely both.

"Good morning again, sleepyhead," Alex whispers.

My hands are still bound. Leather restraints, the kind I've seen in places for crazy folks. Or maybe I saw it in a movie. It's been a while since I've been to a good movie. I saw a preview the other day for that action flick with, shit, what's that actor's name? Kenneth? Keith? Gosh, he has a great voice… *Fuck*, I need to think and keep my wits about me. These drugs are strong.

"Good morning. What happened? I'm having a hard time remembering." Gotta get her talking. Distracted.

"You wanted to know everything. Well…" She opens her arms wide and grins like a schoolgirl. "I'm an open book. I'm all yours. What do you want to know?"

"Start from the beginning. How did this all start?" I slowly tug against my wrists. There is some play in the leather. It might be enough slack to slide my hand out. But what then? She'll get to me before I can free the other hand. Then more drugs? Back into the clouds until I wake up again?

"From the moment I saw you, I loved you. Not just love, Vick, a deep, passionate understanding of love. I desire you. I yearn for you. I obsess over your very name. But all my attempts failed. I tried to get your attention but that cunt wife…" She stops, putting her hand over her mouth and continues "…I'm sorry, I don't mean to offend you, but your *cunt of a wife* got in the way. You were supposed to run into me. *We* were supposed to fall in love; it was never supposed to be *her*."

Are my eyes crossed? I'm trying to pay attention to her words. She rambles about Kraya for a few minutes. Called her a bitch and a peasant. Though I'm not happy with her either, it pisses me off to hear someone else say it.

"My plan was perfect! Well, at least until this deviation…" Alex's fingers slid across my cheek. "In the beginning, I watched you. I wanted to feel close to you. Pretty soon it wasn't enough. I needed to see you everywhere, even when you were working. Every day, every single day, I learned to love you more. Isn't that incredible, Vick?"

"Mmmmmhmmm." Pay attention, dude. Stay alert. Sounds like that song from A-ha, right? Take on me! The one with the sketched video and amazing intro?

♫ *Take on me! Take on me! I'll beeeeee gonnnneeee! In a day or twoooooooooooo!!!!* ♫

Holy shit, pay attention, Vick. How are you going to get out?

She talks for nearly an hour. I'd call it rambling, but she speaks with such poise. I am convinced it could have been three or four years, but the clock on the wall told me otherwise. She was devious. Cunning. She'd spent months working through every angle of what she called her "plan." She always refers to it as "*the* plan." The drugs are wearing off, thank God. I can feel strength growing in my arms again. I tighten my fist and feel the creak of the leather on my wrist.

She'd spent a fortune with her attorneys creating those contracts. Days behind desks reviewing all the intricacies. She planned the Christmas party and the after party *months* in advance. Oh, and I was right about the eBay purchases. She told me she'd *slept with my shirts for months until my smell rubbed off.* Why are the hot ones always so batty? What happened to her? Did you eat a lot of paint chips? Did Daddy touch you?

Then she told me about Kraya. How she'd been slowly poisoning her mind with cocktails of narcotics and medications. She has a key to our home and swapped pills regularly. She'd stolen overdue bills, too, in an effort to make Kraya look irresponsible. That one I noticed, but I thought it was my own doing, not Kray's. She checked our bank balances often, and knew the precise day to contact me for the best probability for a sperm donation.

"Did you really want a baby?" My words are a lot less garbled now.

"Oh, of course! But it has to be real. Real like last night…" Her voice trails and she focused on the ceiling for a long while. Eyes blank, staring into space. It's difficult to see the splendor of the woman I respected, even in awe of, showing her true colors. Alex was a peacock that turned out to be a possum holding up some spray-painted sticks.

"Were the lotto tickets hers? Heroin?"

Alex's sly smile spoke for her. "Guilty!" She raises a playful hand.

"And all of the visits to the clinic for sperm donations? Th... th... the docs? Were they in on it?"

"Carefully planned, Vick. I've spent *so* much time to get you here. I've waited and worked *so* long to be with you. Amazing, isn't it? See how much I love you?"

"Did all the doctors know? The lawyers?" I feel duped — the joke *is* on me and I'm the only fool too dumb to see it.

"No. Gosh, no. I wouldn't trust them not to blow it. I forged some results and spun some believable stories — so many stories, Vick! Can't you see? Every one of those people played a role in my plan. In our plan. And each of them needed a script. I wrote *all* of the scripts. I made all of this possible. Just to be with you."

She kisses me, violently sucking and licking my mouth. It feels gross. Her taste once sweet is now vinegar on my gums. She's stolen something from me that I'll never get back.

She's dangerous. I need to play this right. Or do I? Would it be so terrible to take advantage of her obsession for my own personal gain? She is terrifying, no doubt, but this may work out for me.

"You did all of that…" I pause dramatically, wide-eyed and stupefied — "…for me?"

Alex's grin is so big I can see her top molars. "Yes! I did! Do you love it?"

"I… I think I do. No one has ever done *anything* like this for me. I barely get a birthday card from most people," I said.

"Of course not, Vick. I love you! We're made for each other!" she said, hugging my chest.

"Maybe. But I need more. You know me so well. I need to get to know you. It's only fair."

"Of course! Of course!" She is shaking with excitement. A ball of energy on my lap.

"And these restraints aren't helping our trust here, Alex."

"No? But you know what?" Alex leaned in closely, breathing on my left earlobe, and whispered, "They are good for something…"

I feel warmth in my pants. A hand, I presume, wriggles its way past my waistband. Warm on my bobber as she grips him again.

"You don't have to move, honey." Her whispers are raspy and dirty. She pulls my pants down to my ankles. I feel the heat of her skin on my pelvis. She is slippery, teasing my skin, my arousal involuntary.

"Wait... hold on. Were you even married? Is there an ex-husband?"

She stopped sliding around on my waist. Her glare strong and intentional. "Yes, I was married."

"What happened? Did he really pass away?" I asked.

She pulls off her top and pressed her bare chest to mine. "Yes. He did die..." Alex pulled my shaft upright, sliding herself onto it in a sudden slip. She whispered, "A tragedy, isn't it?" Alex smirked, impaling herself farther down my pole. "I killed him to be with you, Professor." She buried me deeper inside her and tightened around me, gently beginning to bounce. "He died right here." She pointed to the bed with a thin finger. "Right here!" She clenches and spasms. "Right here, baby. I ended him to be with you!" Clawing at my chest — "I did it for you!" She screamed, "I love you, Victor Miller!"

CHAPTER FIFTY-EIGHT
A FEW MONTHS LATER

The bartender tripped over himself to serve her, literally and figuratively. Alex, sporting her hot pink, polka-dotted bikini, ordered two piña coladas. One for me, one for her. The sky was clear, wind quiet, and the sun warm. The pool was one of those cool disappearing edge pools I'd seen in travel magazines. The edge blended perfectly with the ocean. Everyone says it's too cold to swim in the Atlantic, but I'd done it every night anyway. Alex picked our destination. I'd never been to Morocco, and honestly had no idea where it was. We stayed on the north coast, just a skip north of Casablanca, another city I never knew how to find on a map. The resort was beautiful. Three restaurants, four pools, six hot tubs, a helipad, and a cabaret lounge in the lower level. It's one of those rich people destinations that uses names like cottage or villa to describe your room.

We'd been here for nine days already. Our skin was morphing into a golden, peanut butter brown from the countless hours by the pool. It's crazy to think it'd already been two months since we were married. I took a chance, made the best move I could and I'm coming out on top. My buddy, Rob, drafted and delivered the divorce paperwork to Kraya. She signed it in her jail cell, where she awaits trial for possession of heroin, child endangerment, driving under the influence, and a handful of other charges. Rob is watching Junior while we're away. I paid him handsomely, for both the legal help and for watching the wee one.

Alex and I share everything now. It's part of my agreement. I told her I needed access to everything if I am going to trust her. The past is the past, but going forward, I need total transparency and clear access if I'm going to learn to trust her. She agreed. Of course she did. She loves me. She adores me. The amount of painstaking effort she put forth to snag me is incredible. She didn't agree without strings though, no, that would be un-Livingston-like. If I had access to everything, she then needed something to solidify my trust. My son. Legally now *our* son. The adoption paperwork was thicker than the divorce paperwork, but we did it.

After I received the signed copies of the divorce certificate, Alex and I flew to Morocco. We didn't need family or friends. We have each other. Or rather, Alex had me and I have everything Alex has to offer.

She looked stunning walking up the beach in that white dress. We hired a few pretty people as bridesmaids and groomsmen to complete the look. Perfect, soft sand between our toes, a Moroccan priest coaching our vows, and a final kiss to solidify our nuptial.

We celebrated our new union every night with fruity drinks and hot tub romps. I'll hand it to her — she's a good fuck. Very good. Of course she prefers to call it *making love*. So I call it making love now to keep her happy.

She's back with our piña coladas. The wind picked up a bit, blowing the loose towels from our pool chairs and a few stacks of bar napkins into the pool. No other guests bothered us, they couldn't — we booked the entire resort. The staff was bought and tipped before we arrived. Everything was ready before our private jet hit the tarmac.

"It's getting windy!" Alex said, holding her flapping towel.

"It is..." I took the coconut drink and nodded to my new bride with a smile. "Thank you. These things are amazing!" I sip. And sip some more. I can't seem to quench my thirst for booze since I arrived. It's been a tough year. I sucked on the drink until the straw made empty gurgles. Alex hadn't even taken off the paper condom from the top of the straw yet. Her jaw dropped. "You know you're supposed to taste those, right, Professor?"

"Alex. Babe. Seriously? Enough with the *professor* shit."

She parked her ass next to me on my lounge chair. "I know… but it's kinda hot, don't you think? We've been through so much together. It turns me on thinking of you as a professor…" She rims my chest with a finger, biting her lip. Good Lord, woman, does your libido ever run dry?

I take the bait. She looks good and I'm trying my best to learn to love her. I loved her body and coin purse from the get-go, but her mind is going to take some convincing.

Playfully, she pulled me to our villa. Elaborate stone arches and manicured hedges lead us through the maze of our resort. The keycard slid into the cutout above the doorknob and our room unlocked with a buzz. Once inside, Alex pulled the strings dangling from the sides of her bikini. Dainty pieces of swimwear fall to the floor. Blood rushes below my waist. She leaps on top of me, letting out a childish laugh when she lands. "Isn't this wonderful, Vick? Ugh! It's… it's just… things couldn't have turned out better."

"Oh, I don't know. You could have just told me you wanted to run off with me instead of doing all that creepy shit." I got a good chuckle from that one. We've talked through it so many times it was getting repetitive.

We had sex again. Nothing fancy. Missionary with a few edits. She screamed. I screamed. We all screamed for ice cream. I lay back in a sweaty stretch. Alex, equally as sweaty, glistened on the comforter next to me. Her finger traced the scar on my chest.

"Your photoshop skills need help, Alex."

She smirked, dragged her finger along my off-colored patch of skin, and said, "I can't believe I forgot something that simple, something so small. How could I have been so stupid?"

Her expression changed from post-sex-glow to doubt and she turned away from me, facing the stucco wall with the terrible Picasso knock-off. She can be a wee scary. One second, a charmer — a beauty with calculated and perfect conversation. The next, dips, depression, ups and anger. She has problems. Along with those problems, she has millions of green buddies named "Bill" that I am happy to be acquainted with.

"Hey... hey, don't go there again," I said as I sat up. I rested a comforting hand on her bare shoulder. "Everything is awesome, remember? No need to think about the negatives."

"You're right," Alex said, smiling now. She turned back to me and my scar. "You're right. Everything turned out well. I didn't blow it. I didn't screw up the plan. It worked."

I grab her hand with mine and whisper, "The plan is complete. You win! I'm all yours now, Alex. You better take good care of me." I find if I play it cool and work like a snake charmer, she calms down. Her *episodes* have become a regular part of our lives. Like a neighbor's annoying, barking dog you finally learn to ignore.

"You're amazing, Professor! Oh God, I just *love* you! Can you believe we're getting our rings tonight?" It was her idea to have our rings tattooed on our fingers. I expressed my reservations, but eventually I told her I'd do it. "Sickness and health, Professor. Till death do us part."

She popped another bottle of champagne and filled our flutes. I can't tell if the "till death do us part" was a threat, or just Alex being Alex. Either way, I wholeheartedly agreed and took the glass of bubbly with a smirk. Golden bubbles floating up in pretty lines.

"Do you think tonight's the night?" She sipped champagne and wagged her bare bottom all the way to the bathroom. Our villa is a far-too-open floor plan, where the bathroom is wide open to the bedroom, separated only by a few pieces of clear glass. She squatted over the toilet, dripping on the pink stick. She gave me a thumbs-up in unbridled excitement as she waited for the lines to show.

Alex sat a spell, perched expectantly on the toilet. I tossed off the sheets and slid into the hot tub between the living room and bedroom. A major perk of the ever-so-open floor plan is so I can keep an eye on Alex from everywhere. Or maybe that is exactly what she was thinking. Seconds wore on. Minutes. After a while, she got up, wiped her undercarriage, and threw the stick into the trash. Shit. She reeked of disappointment.

After washing her hands in the weird marble sink, Alex joined me in the tub. She snuggled up to me near the strong jets. I smell champagne on her breath and watch a tear roll from her nose. "Baby, it's okay. Next time, right? Practice makes perfect?" She liked that, wiping the tear away with a sniffle and a smile.

"Yeah? You're probably right. People never get pregnant this soon. It may take us a while. And you know what?" Alex pinched my chin. "We have nothing but time." She wrapped her arms around me tightly, like a mother smothering her baby. "You're incredible and patient and wonderful and funny and sweet and brilliant and we're going to get pregnant, Vick."

She kissed me. Her best, last kiss. "You're incredible, too, Alex." I grab her hair with a free hand and plunge her face under the water.

"You're fucking incredible, Alex!" She struggles against my arms. Strong bitch, too. She's able to pull her head out of the water for a quick, loud draw of air. Back into the tub she goes. *Bloop!* Struggling, she flails her arms, kicks her legs, and wriggles her torso like a pissed-off trout.

It took longer than I expected for her to start twitching and stop floating. I hold her under for another minute for good measure. While I wait for her to die good 'n permanent, I sip my champagne. Delicious.

CHAPTER FIFTY-NINE
A FEW MONTHS AGO

"Rob."

"Speaking."

"Rob, we've gotta talk."

"What do you want, dude? Got another sperm contract I need to review?" He laughs into the phone.

"No. Umm, no. Not that easy this time. I need divorce paperwork."

"Vick, stop. I know you're pissed, but it's just a mistake. It has to be."

"Whatever. I don't care. I need divorce paperwork drawn up today."

"No way. It's too late. I need to get home, man."

"I'll pay you a grand. Per page. I need it ASAP. Also, I need a few new marriage docs and child custody forms."

Silence.

"Rob, you there?"

Silence.

"Rob?"

"I'm here. I'm… I'm… just taking it all in. You doing okay? Marriage forms? Custody? For what?"

"Tell you what. Meet me at Phil's so I can sign the forms. It's closer than your office."

"Ohhhhhhh-kayyy? I'll see you there in about an hour. It may take me a bit to get the forms set up."

"Fine. No sweat — long as we can get the divorce finalized ASAP, I'm good."

It took me a few minutes to get to Phil's Tavern. Phil's is the old dive bar next to the highway. It'd been a saloon in the coal mining days and had a reputation for strong drinks and good popcorn. Some people say that place was a brothel in the eighteen hundreds. Those "some people" also sewed drunken stories of Area Fifty-one and government vaccination conspiracies, too.

I left my phone in the car and headed inside. I had a drink. Then another. The third I sipped. I still need at least one or two wits about me. Rob arrived about an hour later. My third drink was dwindling, but still alive.

No foreplay, no chitchat. Rob got right to the point. "Vick, I know you're mad at her. But hear me out..."

"No, hear *me* out, Rob. I don t want to divorce her. I don't. But I found an opportunity for myself and my family that I can't pass up..." I finished drink numero tres and cuatro and started number cinco while I told Rob about Alex. I told him everything. We talked about the sperm donations, the prescription drugs, the heroin, and even the lotto tickets. I discussed her weird perv-room with the six on the door, and I told him every electronic device of mine is to be presumed bugged.

"Ah, that's why you wanted to meet here, not my office. I *knew* something was up." He slapped his hand on the table and swigged his bourbon. He spilled a few drops of booze on the divorce paperwork and certificate, wiping them up with a sloppy, drink-ringed bar napkin.

"Look through these when you get home." I slid a thumb drive across the table to him. "I will still need the divorce though. And a marriage certificate, a child custody release, and adoption and a few other forms."

"I don't quite understand, buddy," Rob said. He lifted the thumb drive from the table and looked at it curiously.

"Good. Then you won't be an accessory." I slammed the rest of drinko cinco, signed the divorce forms and anything else that had a yellow "Sign Here!" arrow. I slid on my coat and told him I'd call him. He told me he would email whatever other forms I need ASAP and get the certificates notarized.

"Hey, Rob? Check the thumb drive. Make sure the right people get it."

CHAPTER SIXTY
PRESENT

I took a moment to collect myself. Alex had been floating around on the bubbling surface of the hot tub for ten minutes. She was dead, leaving behind the hull of a vixen. Or maybe, the soup of a vixen? Though I'm not sure if it qualifies as soup because there aren't noodles or peas or anything.

I called the front desk and did my best impression of a frantic honeymooner. It didn't take long for sirens and uniforms to come bursting into the room. Medics, docs, and police officers all paced around the room. Some looked at me with empathy, others with suspicion.

They called an interpreter because I don't speak Arabic and they barely spoke English, and since a dead chick is floating around like a terrible game of bobbing for apples, they needed the story to be communicated clearly and correctly.

"I-I-I-I was just with her, and when I came back from the shower, she was like this. I-I-I-I tried to give her CPR, but I couldn't get… *(moan with a hint of a sob)* I couldn't get her back!" I said with more academy-award crying.

The smell of alcohol was strong on her breath as the medics pumped on her dead, naked chest. The bartender corroborated my story, telling them that we'd been drinking like fish since we arrived. He told them we seemed happy. No fighting, just lots of fucking. The hotel staff heard our cries of glee throughout the villa gardens.

I hoped that would work. For days I'd been moaning so loud my windpipes were sore. In another effort to make us appear to be innocently love stricken, I scattered love notes around the room, but none of the cops even saw them. Or maybe none of them wanted to do the paperwork for more evidence. Either way, someone must have told them it looked good enough to be ruled an accidental drowning of a drunk broad. In the States, this would have been investigated for months, but not here. Her "riches" didn't raise a single eyebrow. Over here, her many millions were nothing compared to the oil baron billions with a "b."

"I didn't know she was *that* drunk! My… (sob) *my wife!*"

Accented apologies from everyone who walked by me. I sat on the bed. Crying sometimes, drinking the rest. More medics. A coroner. More cops, some in suits instead of the unitard. They also ruled it accidental. I was stunned. How ridiculous was this? I was so sure I would spend a few days in their weird, Middle Eastern jail before they realized there just wasn't enough evidence to put me away.

They had me sign a bunch of forms: a coroner's report, a letter of investigation, extradition releases, certificate of death, and a few other things I barely read. My eyes were too puffy to keep reading. The tack I'd placed on my ass cheek was working. Maybe too well. That sucker hurt. Every time I moved it poked into the same, tortured hole in my bum skin. It didn't hurt nearly enough to cry, but it sure made it easier to remember how to do it.

One of the detectives told me how sorry he was this happened to me on my honeymoon. He then hummed something in Arabic and shook my hand. He told me it was a prayer to help me through my loss. I thanked him and told him it was beautiful.

Finally, after six long, exhausting hours, after all the photos were taken, forms signed, statements made and quiet conversations had been had, they wheeled her body out of the room and left me alone.

CHAPTER SIXTY-ONE

Setting up a return flight to the States was simple. People answer your call at any hour when you have money to burn. I waited at the airport in a private lounge. I watched them load the plane with my bags and the casket. The casket wasn't fancy either, just a cedar box with a few Arabic symbols on the top. I hadn't had lunch yet, so I tried the tagine, a cocktail of beef and rice and other submerged mysteries of the East. Not bad really. Tasted like an oddly spiced Asian dish.

The machine they used to load her body into the plane drove away and I got twinges of regret. Okay, maybe not regret — guilt? Did I need to kill her? Remember, she tried to kill Kraya or at least made her want to die. She tore my family apart. I couldn't give her a pass — right? I had to do something — I needed to. It was required to keep them safe from future Alex freak-outs. It also didn't hurt that I finagled this thing in my financial favor. She was vulnerable and I had an edge — so sue me.

I boarded the jet and was alone in the cabin except for a couple of appealing flight attendants. Just the crew and me for this flight. The pilots were nice, too. A bunch of apologies for my loss followed by one of those gentle, heartwarming, double-handed handshakes. I chose to sit near the TV. I've seen my share of clouds, no need to gawk at them like a fat kid's first day at the amusement park.

I had a glass of what I assumed to be expensive red wine before takeoff. Even though I'm not a wine guy, it was delicious. I think it's against the rules to drink wine quickly, but I did it anyway. The busty Asian gal in the flight attendant romper was quick to pour another.

At thirty thousand feet, the pilot addressed me by name, telling me a few facts about the flight and asked if I needed anything, I can ask the ladies or walk up and open the door to talk with them. Security isn't an issue with private planes. These guys know that you spent five or six digits to fly for a few hours and there are cheaper, less terrifying ways a rich guy can meet his maker.

I pulled a small, folded piece of paper from my wallet. I started at number one on the list and picked up the phone from the wooden desk next to my seat. I called Rob. He answered professionally because he didn't recognize my number.

"Vick? Holy shit! It's been what, a few months? What is going on?"

"Hey, buddy. We can catch up when I get back; I need you to do a few things for me. First thing, did it work?"

"It worked. It wasn't as easy as I thought it would be. The judge did some digging and released her. He didn't believe the recording of Alexa at first, so he had a detective sniff around her apartment. Dude found a bunch of the stuff you guys were talking about in the recording. Oh, Alexa is fucked all right. He issued a warrant right away," Rob said.

"Uh, yeah… That's great. So Kraya's well? No lingering criminal charges?" I replied. The thumb drive with my recorded conversations with Alex did the trick. I was always so nervous she would figure out I was recording her confessions. If she did figure it out, who knows what she'd do or what she'd be capable of.

"No charges, pal. She is doing fine. It took her a few weeks to get back to her old self. Docs wanted her to take a few medications for the stress, but she's been flying cold turkey. She doesn't trust anything that even looks like a pill!"

"I don't blame her. Tell her I'll be home soon."

"She can't wait for this to be over."

"Me, too. Just a few things first. I need you to clear the P.O.A. at the bank. I'm sending it... now." I attached the power of attorney to an email and clicked *send*.

"Annnnd..." He paused for a few seconds. "Got it."

"File that as soon as possible. I need access before I land," I said.

"Yeah, that's great and all, but Alexa will void this once she figures out you're trying to convert her accounts," Rob said, concern in his voice.

"Alex passed away, Rob. Tragic hot tub accident."

The line was quiet. I couldn't hear his gears turning, but I'm sure they were. "You still there?" Although my flight was more expensive than some small homes, the connection was, at times, echoey and untrustworthy.

"Yeah, man. I'm here. Just taking it all in."

"Good. Don't think too hard, Rob. We have work to do."

"All right. I'll submit these. Anything else?"

I'm glad he asked. In addition to the power of attorney, I needed several of her account beneficiary tags activated, some life insurance paperwork submitted, and estate cash accounts transferred. I sent him a few more emails and he received them. His emails and conversation were more reserved once I'd told him of the untimely death of my second wife. I think it scared him. Can't blame 'em — sounds spooky. I'll make time to smooth it over with him, and he will know whatever he wants to know soon enough. But not now. No time to worry about Rob. I have a long list and only a few business hours to get things done because of the time change. It was still breakfast time here, but it was edging up on early afternoon stateside.

Farther down the list I found the scribbled number of Routine Movers, LLC, a company I'd prepped before I left. I called and spoke with Mike again. He sounded like a middle-aged smoker from Boston who'd been eating pizza rolls for thirty years. Nice enough guy though. He told me they can move my appointment up, but it would add an extra *"Four grand, for you know, overnight work..."* I gave him the approval he needed and the codes to my new apartment in Livingston Tower. Alex's old apartment. I also reminded Mike to trash all the shit in room six. No questions. No answers. Just throw everything away. I'm sure he'll keep the computers and maybe the watch, but I don't care. Hell, this guy might even keep a few of the dildos if he's into that sort of thing. All I care is that it is gone. Forever gone.

I set the delivery address to Luxury Estate Sales and Auctions. Another one I found from a quick Google search. I called Morty, a quirky auctioneer with the sniffles, and told him I had an apartment full of luxury stuff to sift through. He confirmed the delivery address, payment instructions, and bid me adieu.

Next, I called my bank and about ten other offices and financial institutions. Everyone was surprisingly indifferent about Alex's death. Was just another day at the office for these bankers, attorneys, and insurance agents. What a pleasant bunch. My fingers were lightning on the keyboard, emailing docs and filling out forms. Everyone got the information they needed before 5 p.m., Central Standard Time. For me it's probably still 8 a.m., MFA, otherwise known as 8 a.m. — Middle of the Fucking Atlantic ocean time zone.

For the first time in months, I leaned back in my chair, closed my eyes, and fell asleep without a head full of anxiety. Yeah, sure. I killed Alex, but she fucked with my wife. She fucked with my son. She fucked with me. She was begging for it. Besides, I bet she is more relaxed now, too. Cramped, but relaxed.

CHAPTER SIXTY-TWO

It was still dark when we touched down. It was so smooth I barely noticed we landed. I like flying private. Good food, great wine, pleasant staff — what a treat. It also helped that there weren't any annoying, bouncing teenagers from Ohio on the flight. Local police met me on the tarmac holding rifles and frowns. Surprise!

Fuck. Fuck. *Fuck. They know. I knew I shouldn't have submitted the life insurance that fast. Fuck!* As the plane came to a soft stop, they surrounded the plane. A few SUVs and a bunch of black and whites; their red and blue lights flickered brightly against the night.

I asked for another shooter of that fancy wine and Asia was happy to fill my glass. Damn that's good wine. May be my last taste of freedom and wine for a good while.

The crew opened the door, letting in the strange smells of engines and fresh air. The stairs dropped to the concrete tarmac and up came the platoon of uniformed, American police officers. These guys were so much different than the Moroccan police. I bet the stubble on the first officer's face could beat up one of the Moroccan sergeants.

"Mr. Victor Miller?" Officer Boose asked.

"Yes?" I said.

"Victor…"

Oh fuck, here it comes!

"Miller, we have an arrest warrant…"

Shit!

"…for Alexa Lee Livingston, a.k.a. Alexa Lee Miller. Is she on board this plane? We were told she would be."

Holy hell, are you kidding me, fellas? "Yeah, umm. Yes…" I needed a bit of ham for this one. Not as in, cops and pork joke ham, as in hamming it up. *(Sniffle)* "She is in the cargo hold, Officer." I let out a wheeze and another sniffle. "She died." I lost it. Almost a laugh, but I caught myself and started crying. I'd like to thank God, my wife, and my son for this award for outstanding theatrical performance.

"Sir. I'm sorry to hear that, but we're going to need to search the plane anyway."

Ass. He put me in handcuffs. Hell, they put everyone on the plane in handcuffs. They went as far as opening the casket and matching the picture from the DMV. Had this been a woman I loved, I would have been pissed. My theatrics continued. I sobbed, contained myself, cried, and then just sat there, stone faced and exhausted. Again, some serious trophy material.

They apologized, reviewed my death certificates, and popped off the handcuffs with a click. They told me I'd need to send the death certificate to a judge by Monday or they will probably keep showing up looking for her. I told him I would. They told me about her warrant, and that she was being charged with fraud, poisoning with intent, burglary, grand theft, stalking, kidnapping, and a bunch of other good stuff. Rob, buddy, you done good. The recording of Alex was enough to wipe Kray's slate clean and curse Alex's. The cops gave me some business cards and left. They didn't know I was the one behind it all. They were just the chubby chumps in charge of bagging the crook.

What a week. I have faced, and evaded, two sets of police departments on different continents. Is it really *that* easy? In their defense, these last dudes weren't looking for a murder suspect, they were looking to serve a warrant. And the Moroccan guys didn't give a shit about another snotty American tourist. I should be careful though. I may not be as lucky if there is a third strike.

After the adrenaline wore off, I dragged my luggage across the runway to my waiting car, a black sedan with a bodyguard-sized driver. The reservation was another one of the calls I made in the air. He was leaning against the black Lincoln in a well-fitting suit. His shoes were scuffed and he had a five-o'clock shadow, but you could tell he meant business.

I greeted him with a handshake and asked, "Nick Kage, with a K?" It was going to be fun to say that I had Nick Kage driving me around, even if he wasn't the guy from *Face Off*.

"That's, me. You Vick? Victor Livingston?"

"You're half right. I'm Victor *Miller*, and we're going to Livingston Tower."

"Yeah, crap. I get my notes mixed up sometimes," he said, hitting himself on the side of the head with a wide palm.

Nice enough guy. Good driver, too. Maybe a smidge on the slow side though. Not the Floridian old lady behind the wheel slow, the other kind of slow. But how smart do you have to be to pick me up from the airport and wait for me outside Livingston Tower? He closed the door behind me with a hushed thud. No jet engines. No police. No conversation — just the back of the quiet town car. I pulled out my phone and called Rob.

"Good morning, Rob!"

"Dude. Do you know what time it is?"

"Is that a serious question?"

"Oh shit. (Yawn) I must have forgotten the alarm…" I could hear him fumbling to get out of bed, his wife grumbling in the background. "I'll meet you there in about an hour. Does that still work?"

"Yeah, that's fine. Kray and Little Man going to be there?" Friggen' Rob. Guy could sleep through a trainado (What, you've never heard of a tornado full of trains?)

"Of course. They're so excited to see you."

"Good. Me, too. See you soon."

I hung up and slipped my phone into my jacket pocket. Just a few more stops. First, we parked in front of Manhattan Mutual and Trust. I'd requested a banker to open early, just for me, to finalize the fund transfers. I walked into the echoing, marble-filled bank and met the only person there. All of the offices were dark, except for one — his. It was chilly in the bank, too.

Mr. Peterstorf guided me to his office with a pleasant gesture and greeting. I made a joke about the bank being empty and he looked at me with lifeless eyes and laughed. He responded with a comment about coffee, and how there is never enough. We made a few more attempts at small talk, but failed miserably because of his sense of humor (or lack thereof). It was hard to be funny or awake this early in the morning. Or does it still qualify as late at night? This guy was running on fumes.

He verified my transfer requests and scanned copies of my ID and other certificates. It was part of my deal with Alex that I would have access to everything. All of her computers, documents, and of course, all of her money. She's a smart girl though. She gave me access to a few of her accounts when we were married. Armed with a death certificate, a will, a power of attorney, and a few other complicated-looking documents, I'm now the sole owner of her fortune. All of it, not just the accounts she wanted me to know about.

I transferred just over eight million to my savings account. I also created two, ten million dollar CDs, with almost all of the interest funneling into two checking accounts. I transferred the remainder to a separate, new account. On the flight, I'd finalized a trust, ensuring my family would always have this money, with limited taxes, as long as the trust entity existed. The principal amount in the trust would never be touched. The interest, however, could be collected by my future heirs.

I signed a stack of paper while Mr. Peterstorf hid a yawn and drank his coffee.

CHAPTER SIXTY-THREE

Livingston Tower was the last stop before I finally meet Kraya and my son again. This was a place I hoped to never see again. I'm sure Alex's pop is going to be quite upset when he finds out I drained all of her accounts. But what can he do now? I don't own most of the money anymore anyway, my trust does. He can sue me, take me to court, harass me, and steal the pennies from my change jar, but it won't change the fact that he will never get her money back. Besides, it's her money, not his. And now it's mine — her grieving widower's dowry.

Livingston Tower was quite dark at this hour. A few offices were aglow, but most were waiting until normal business hours to flip on the bulbs. I'm sure her father and mother are up there somewhere, too, sobbing into their huge pillows. Heck, I would, too, if it were my kid.

I recognized the cluster of faces behind the lobby counter. They said pleasant hellos and let me walk by. No one is rushing to get into a conversation with her widower. Not tonight anyway.

I punched one-one-three-zero into the elevator and took it to her floor. When the doors opened, it wasn't as it usually looked. Once a pristine hallway, adorned with freshly waxed marble and wood stain so dark it looked English, now looked like a construction site. Her door was propped open with a crumpled soda can and plastic sheets lined the tile, protecting the flooring from the all-night event of gruff movers. Nothing was left inside her place. Literally nothing, not even the appliances. All of her belongings are gone. All of her furniture, gone. Those bottles of red wine, gone. Her old place is now a shell of who she once was. Just like her, I suppose.

In a big, brown trash barrel I found a few remnants of the room, the creepy room with the number on the door. Some torn-up pictures and a few computer screens. Turns out the guys listened to me after all. The computers had been crushed and tossed into this barrel. My old jacket, some odd knickknacks I didn't recognize — everything. The windows were exposed now, too. No more foil covering, protecting her peculiar room from sunlight. It's a nice, quaint office space now. I bet the next owner will put a desk over there and have cocktails while they pay their bills or surf porn like a normal person. I pulled the number six off one of two nails on the door and threw it into the waste bin.

I checked the other rooms, too. Utterly and relievingly empty. The bedroom, where we shared one good time and many terrifying ones, was just a few scratches and furniture dents in the floor. Only the smell of her perfume lingered. I felt an odd jolt of terror and arousal. I checked the living room, office, kitchen, and closet. All barren. All of her shit is in a box truck, doing sixty-five mph on the interstate by now, headed to auction. These guys must have spent all night pulling down pictures and carrying sofas to the elevator. Pictures... gross. Pictures of me.

I did one last pass through the apartment before I locked the door. The cupboards were empty, silverware gone. These guys even threw out the toilet paper. The apartment will go on the market tomorrow. My realtor should have already taken pictures and prepped the listing. I could sell it myself, but I'd rather leave it to a professional and be done with this turd.

I stop into her shrine room one last time. I flick out the light with my left hand and close the door. In that moment before the light emptied from the room, I saw something. Something far under the desk in the corner, a brownish yellow-tinged curiosity.

I turned the light back on and crouch beneath the built-in desk. I stretch an arm under the longest corner and grab what I initially thought to be a tiny liquor bottle. But it wasn't.

It's not booze at all. It's a new, sealed, bottle of vanilla extract. Strange place for some cooking ingredient to live, but whatever. I walk out of the room that once had a six on the door, turn off all the lights in her apartment, lock the front door, and slide the vanilla into my pocket.

I'll keep the vanilla. It's Saturday night and Kraya has cookies to bake.

Thank you for reading Alex Six!
If you love it...
Please please please leave a review
On Goodreads & Amazon!
...AND TELL YOUR FRIENDS!
It is SO helpful! -Vince Taplin

Made in the USA
Coppell, TX
06 September 2020

37093881R10187